Rachel and the Fair Folk

Dominic Miles

ISBN 9781973264156

Chapter 1

The body lay on the slab in front of her for all the world like a marble statue from a museum heist. It wasn't like any other dead body she had ever seen and, over these past years, there had been more than a few of them.

Rachel never liked this part of the job. On the slab, the human body was revealed in all its frail vulnerability. You couldn't avoid seeing yourself lying there or someone dear to you. It made you so aware of your own mortality, the fragile nature of life. But this one was different. It really was like a statue, lacking that extraordinary quality that corpses have, because even the lack of life does not completely rob people of their humanity.

"I haven't seen one of these before," Mr. Roberts said. He was always Mr. Roberts, never Tony. Though he thought nothing of calling her Rachel, rather than D.S. Stevens.

"Well, not one like this," he quickly corrected himself, because a corpse was a corpse after all, however exotic.

The body was slim, well-muscled and defined. It was male – very male, Rachel thought, glancing at the genitals – but the skin was dead-white and waxy. Dead bodies often had that waxy quality she knew, but it was quite pronounced in this one and the skin was also very smooth and unblemished.

He had long hair which was of a greyish shade, even though he seemed to be in his thirties or forties, with none of the wrinkles or sagging skin that were the minute and stealthy signs of age. He had a longish nose, arched eyebrows, and eyes of a fading greenish tinge. In short, his face had an otherworldly look, made even more outlandish by his ears. They were, to be frank, decidedly pointy.

"What do you make of those, Tony?" Rachel asked, knowing that by using his first name she would irritate the older man. Mr. Roberts frowned, but he didn't take her bait. He was too confused by what he was seeing to get into an argument with her about titles.

"Plastic surgery, I think," he said. "There was a spate of it some years ago, when the Lord of the Rings films were coming out. People were going and getting elf ears from private clinics. Quite unethical really, but not illegal. One step up from tattooing or body piercing."

Rachel noticed something about Mr. Roberts. He might be his usual arrogant self on the surface, doling out sarcasm in his public-school tones, dressed to give a subtle intimation of class and status in his tweed jacket and those terrible red trousers that only the county set wear, but underneath it all he was nervous and somewhat preoccupied. He'd come up against something he didn't understand and was grasping at straws, trying to explain it away.

"Alien, I would think," Mr. Roberts muttered.

"Alien?" Rachel picked up on the word. "Extra-terrestrial?" She asked, smiling as she said it. It did, after all, seem a lame explanation.

"No, I mean alien in the sense of foreign!" Mr. Roberts answered, quickly.

Then why not say foreign, Rachel thought, or from abroad, or something, not bloody alien.

"Slavic, I think, looking at the high cheek bones, so Russian or East European. To all intents and purposes, a fine example of a human specimen in early middle age."

He paused, making another quick appraisal of the body.

"I'll have to open him up of course," he smiled with a certain amount of relish as he said this, but Rachel thought that it was only natural. It was his job after all. We should all enjoy our jobs, shouldn't we?

"Because," Roberts added, "there's no mark or sign on him which would suggest how he died. Run the circumstances by me again!"

She didn't catch what he meant at first, but then, realising, she retrieved her note book from her handbag and read.

"He was found in an alley off the Caledonian Road. He was lying on the pavement and the woman who found him though he was a drunk sleeping it off at first."

Rachel screwed her eyes up trying to read her own writing, either she was going to have to make a conscious effort not to scrawl her words, or she was going to have to buy reading glasses.

"He was dressed in an expensive-looking suit, but there were no labels or any identifying marks on it. Similarly, his shoes looked hand-crafted, not your usual Clarks anyway. He had no wallet, no credit cards and no mobile phone."

"Unusual to have nothing on him," Roberts said.

"He could have been mugged, of course, or more likely his body was rifled before our member of the public found him. It's unlikely anyone would take his shoes or clothes, but anything else would be up for grabs and his fingers seem to have those indentations on them. You know, like those you get when you wear a wedding ring."

Rachel once had personal knowledge of this, she'd worn a wedding ring, but that was some years ago.

"Very good!" Roberts said, in such a patronising way that it made Rachel wince.

"Look here!" He said, leaning over the dead man's head. "His ears were pierced as well, on both sides. He may have had ear rings too, which might also have been taken, though there's no trauma around the lobes."

Rachel looked at the dead man's ears, like two flattened, convoluted sea shells.

"There's no sign of scarring," she said.

"What do you mean?" Roberts asked, somewhat defensively.

"Well, if he'd had plastic surgery, as you say, wouldn't there be some sign of scarring?"

"That was just a supposition on my part, Rachel," Roberts answered, still on his guard, "but perhaps it was done with skill and he healed well. Who knows?"

Or, Rachel thought, he was born with pointy ears, but she didn't say it out loud. Mr. Roberts was irritable at the best of times and he was growing more uncomfortable as time went on.

"Well, I won't be starting the autopsy tonight," he said, looking at his watch.

"Got a prior engagement?" Rachel asked getting a glare from Roberts in return.

"It's nearly eight o'clock, D.S. Stevens," he answered. He always reverted to using her rank, when he was cross with her. "Our friend can wait for the morning."

Rachel looked down at the body. It was true, he wasn't going anywhere.

Rachel phoned Ellen to say that she would be late. It was just a courtesy really, not a question of emotional investment. Rachel knew that Ellen would cook something for them both, so it was just polite to tell her she was delayed and Ellen could put it in the oven for later. She was getting better at this sort of thing, what other people called being considerate. It was bad enough having to share a flat with someone else when she was in her forties, but that was being single in London. Housing costs were astronomical and it was only the millionaires who could afford a decent place. Even on a D.S.'s salary she was struggling, though it was true that she'd never been good with money. When she was married she'd done the whole setting-up-a-house thing, but they'd never got a mortgage, because Al didn't want to be tied down. He wanted to travel, make something of his life. In the end he didn't do either. He was selling cars somewhere north of Finchley and living with some vacuous, air-headed twenty- something, all tits and arse. Not that she was bitter, of course.

She got back to the station at 8.30pm. She still had the paper work to do on the mystery man and a few other things to get done before the morning. Policing was all paper work these days and she'd never been one of the bookish ones at school. It had always been sports with her and athletics. She'd been encouraged by her P.E. teachers, because, as everyone knew, black girls could run, couldn't they?

She'd done well enough, as it turned out, got into university and then into the police, but she'd never been an academic. And now there were all these high-fliers coming into the force, with their masters' degrees and Ph.Ds. All writing articles about criminology and sociology. Not much room for old-style coppers in the force these days.

Rachel made coffee, just to keep herself going, and settled down at her desk, switching the desk light and the P.C. on. Her division was housed in a Victorian building in Holloway, with an ancient lift that never worked, a canteen that should have been condemned back in the 1930s – along with the canteen staff – and bathrooms that were probably fitted out by Thomas Crapper himself. The toilets, in fact, were the only part of the building that was worth preserving, with their ceramic, patterned tiles and their intricate wrought iron fittings.

There was no one else in the building, no-one else except D.C. Thomas, who seemed to be a permanent fixture. Though he didn't appear to get out of the office much, and was one of those time-servers who were near retirement and not the most dynamic of coppers. He was always loath to go home to his wife and his drove of kids – four or five, Rachel thought, by the last count – and his reluctance to embrace family life had become a bit of an office joke.

Seeing Rachel, he nodded a greeting to her and said:

"I think I've got something for you."

Thomas disappeared and then emerged with an evidence bag that someone hadn't yet booked in.

"Sergeant Ryan and P.C. Williams did a stop and search on two kids off the Caledonian Road a few hours ago. They were acting suspiciously."

Rachel knew what he really meant. Ryan and Williams, both white, had stopped a couple of black kids on some pretext. It happened all the time, it went with the territory, as they said, but it still left a bad taste in Rachel's mouth. She'd grown up in a white middle-class suburb of Oxford and any racism that she'd encountered had been subtle and covert. Oxford was cosmopolitan enough for a mixed-race kid like her to have a reasonable childhood, but if she'd grown up on the Caledonian Road she knew things would have been different.

The thing was, though, and you had to admit it, lots of these kids were either involved in gangs or scared of them and so they went armed. Knives mainly, guns were few and far between but not unknown, and while you did come across the hefty, zombie-killer blades, more like military weapons than anything else, a lot of the kids carried kitchen knives or sharpened screw drivers. Small blades that were easily concealed.

Whatever the wrongs and rights of it, Thomas was now holding out the evidence bag so she could see. The kids, fourteen and fifteen years old respectively, had apparently admitted that they had taken the items off an unconscious body. It was probably an act of bravado, as it turned out that they had little idea what they were going to do with their haul.

"Weird stuff," Thomas said and he showed her a number of silver rings, a pair of silver earrings and a pendant of some sort.

"That's not all!" He said, producing a small leather pouch and pouring its content onto the table. "Gold coins! You don't see this kind of stuff every day!"

Thomas emailed the boys' statements to Rachel. The two of them had been co-operative. They were good boys, good students, cousins and when their mothers had turned up to take them home - two formidable sisters who were stalwarts of their local church and took their bible literally – they'd told Ryan and Williams everything. The description of the unconscious man they'd taken their loot from matched the description of her dead body.

"Oh, by the way," Thomas said. "I took the liberty of doing some research on the symbols etched into the rings."

Rachel hadn't noticed these designs, but with her attention drawn to them, she could make out the spirals and whorls of the patterns.

"They are apparently of Celtic origin. I've tracked down similar examples of these designs on rings and other jewelry dating to the Dark Ages."

Rachel had known that Thomas was a history buff, it was a hobby he was keeping warm until his retirement, but she wasn't so enthusiastic about the past.

"When was the Dark Ages?" She asked.

Thomas smiled condescendingly.

"To give you some idea, between the time the last Roman Legions left and the Saxon kingdoms emerged. Approximately 500AD to 1000AD."

"Well that narrows it down," Rachel said, with a sarcasm that went completely over Thomas' head, and then quickly added a question.

"So, are we looking at some sort of dealer in antiquities?"

"Well, we could be," Thomas answered, "but by all accounts, he was wearing them!"

Chapter 2

Ellen was still up when Rachel got home. She was marking books; such was the lot of secondary school teachers, up till all hours. Gone were the days when teaching was a six-hour day with long holidays. Why did everything get worse, Rachel wondered, not better?

They did not have much to say to each other, but sat in companiable silence, when Ellen finished her marking, watching the TV. They were like an old married couple, Rachel thought. Ellen tended to do the cooking, though not exclusively, they shared the housework and they invariably spent their evenings together falling asleep on the settee in front of the blue glow of the screen. There was usually, also, a bottle of wine open, though Ellen would often have just one glass leaving Rachel to finish it off. It was one way, if not the best, of dealing with the stress of the job.

Yes, Rachel thought, they were like a married couple, apart from the fact, of course, that they didn't sleep together, which probably made it the perfect marriage. Get sex out of the way and what had you got? Mutual companionship and fewer arguments. They both had failed relationships behind them, though they didn't talk about them. In fact, Rachel didn't know what gender Ellen's significant other had been. She had mentioned the name Kerry – or Kerrie or Ceri - on occasion – usually in a negative context, but the name could be male or female and Rachel had never pursued the matter.

Rachel didn't care. She got along well enough with Ellen and she couldn't say that about many people. Leave the sharing of feelings and mutual navel-gazing to other people and fall back on good, old British reserve, she thought. These days too many people spilled their guts out to other people, over the dinner table or over the Internet.

Eventually they'd dragged themselves off to their separate beds and Rachel had woken up next morning to an all-enveloping shit storm, a veritable blizzard of the stuff.

She was hardly out of the shower before her mobile rang. It was Thomas, conveying a message from Roberts. The body had gone.

"What do you mean gone?" She'd asked, bad-temperedly. One of Rachel's more unenviable qualities was a tendency to blame the messenger.

"I'm just telling you what he said," Thomas retorted. "Someone broke in and stole the body!"

"Burke and Hare, I presume!" Rachel said, but Thomas, though he was history buff, didn't quite get the reference.

It took her about thirty minutes to get to the morgue, the traffic was, as usual, backed up and she had to zigzag through the suburban streets and squares. Roberts was standing outside when she pulled up in the hospital car park.

"They came through the side door," he said. "The fire exit. It's pretty sturdy, so it's a wonder to me how they got through without some sort of machinery. A drill or something."

He said the word "machinery" with a distasteful tone in his voice, as if such manual work was somehow beneath him.

"It was opened from the inside," Rachel said, after examining it. "It's a fire door and there's no sign of it being forced and it can only be opened from the inside."

"But how can that be?" Roberts asked. "There was no-one working. The place was all locked up. There's twenty-four-hour access of course, but only by punching in a code. They must have got in through here somehow and come out the same way."

Rachel wasn't going to argue with him, she knew that even the best electronic security measures could be compromised and, besides, the how wasn't as interesting to her as the why.

"Are there any CCTV cameras?" She asked.

The CCTV cameras were controlled centrally, in a windowless room somewhere in the bowels of the hospital. It seemed to take an inordinate amount of time for the security guard, a prime example of the can't-really-be-arsed school of public servant, to scroll through the digital records and come up with the relevant clip.

She was none the wiser when she'd seen it. An anonymous van parked outside the morgue, two men in overalls, their faces obscured, loading up a long, suspicious-looking box. The side door wasn't covered by a camera, but the entrance lobby was and it seemed that no-one had gained entry that way.

"Didn't anybody check out this van?" She asked the security guard, one of those gray, anonymous, middle-aged men that the world was full of, but he shrugged and said:

"We can't note all the comings and goings in the hospital. This place is busy around the clock."

Rachel had thought that that was the whole point of having security guards, but she didn't say anything.

"Besides," he added, "the alarm didn't go off!"

That was another mystery, not only how they got in, but why the alarm system didn't work.

She requisitioned a copy of the tapes, found a coffee shop in the foyer, one of those international coffee chains that had spread their tentacles into hospitals, banishing the WRVS tea trolley, and bought a take-out coffee and a sandwich – more expensive than the supermarket, but she wouldn't have time to stop anywhere else – and was heading back to the station when she got the call.

She pulled off the Caledonian Road, onto one of those non-descript side roads, lined with terraced houses that had seen better days and had the untidy look of dwellings in multiple occupation, gardens crammed with bins or old white goods, rubbish bags piled on the streets, paint peeling off facades.

There was an old guy called Phillips, who used to be the caretaker at the station until he retired some years ago. He was always banging on about how these neighbourhoods had once been solid working-class places where you could leave your back door open and not worry about your neighbours. Well, those days were long gone. There were whole streets now that were blighted, buildings falling down, people falling apart, until some developer came and turned them into town houses and luxury apartments, driving out the people who'd lived there all their lives, pricing them out of the market.

At the end of the road was an old Working Men's Institute, which hadn't been used as such for something like a hundred years, but instead had gone through various evolutions as a pub and then as various clubs. It had been notorious in the fifties for being the haunt of the Maltese gangs that ruled London at the time, until they were displaced by people like the Krays, and these days its reputation was no better. Though it went by the name of 'Havana Nights', locals knew it as the 'Hav' and it was notorious as a place where you could get a drink downstairs and a massage upstairs. And when they said massage, they weren't talking about a luxury spa experience.

As she pulled up, she could see her brethren from the armed response unit on the streets around the place, but they looked relaxed, off-guard, so she knew that whatever had gone down had already happened. Her boss, D.I. Andrews was in front of the building in conversation with one of the ARU guys. He nodded to her as she approached. Andrews was called Haggis behind his back for two reasons; firstly, because he was Scottish; and secondly because most of the detectives she worked with behaved as if they were adolescents.

"Sir," she said, as she approached.

"Hi, Rachel," Andrews answered. "You're never going to believe this one."

Somebody had called in a disturbance at the club. It was an anonymous call. When the ARU had got there, they had found the doors wide open, the windows broken and half a dozen dead or seriously injured men downstairs. Upstairs, the girls had ether barricaded themselves into their rooms, or hidden in cupboards and closets. Whichever way they had secreted themselves, they were all now semi-hysterical.

They hadn't seen a gangland killing like this in the division for some time, all of ten years, and to put something of a cap on it, all of the dead and injured had been either hacked about with long-bladed instruments or shot with arrows.

"So," Andrews said, when he had finished briefing her. "It looks like they were attacked with swords and crossbows. Rather a novel approach!"

The ARU Inspector looked uncomfortable at Andrews's words.

"Well, definitely crossbows, but you could be talking about machetes, rather than swords as such. The sort of thing the Yardies use." He said.

"The wounds are too regular for machetes," Andrews said. "And some of those guys were stabbed, not hacked!"

The SOCOs were doing their work on the ground floor, but Rachel booted and suited up and climbed the stairs to the first floor where a couple of woman constables were trying to interview the girls.

"Hi Sarge," one of the officers said as Rachel entered into the hallway. Rachel knew her; her name was Sam. She was one of those young, enthusiastic types who would probably go far, as long as she kept her nose clean and turned a blind eye when it was called for.

"How's it going, Sam?" Rachel asked.

"Not too well. It's like the United Nations up here. Russians, Vietnamese, you name it. Some of them are probably trafficked, if not all of them. We'll have to take them down the station and arrange for interpreters as most of them don't speak much English. They can just about ask the customers if they want a 'happy ending' but not much more. And those who do speak English, won't! Nobody's talking about what happened."

It turned out to be a long, dreary afternoon's work, all those women to process, interpreters to be arranged, interviews carried out. The murder would be handed over to a Major Incident Team, but for the time being there was plenty to be done.

Rachel was late home and for once Ellen was out. It wasn't until she got to the flat that Rachel remembered that Ellen had told her she wouldn't be there. She couldn't be bothered to cook, so she ordered in a pizza; she was almost too tired to eat it.

She was dozing on the sofa when the phone rang.

"Sorry to call you at home," said a voice. It was Andrews. "But I don't think this can wait."

Rachel tried to wake up and listen to him.

"I think there's a connection between the killings and the body that went missing, but I want to keep it between you and me for now. It's a bit sensitive."

This wasn't like Andrews, Rachel thought, he usually did everything by the book. He was scrupulous about it.

"I want you to go and talk to someone," he said.

"What? Now, Sir?" Rachel asked.

"No, tomorrow," Andrews replied. "And pack a bag, you'll be away for at least one night."

Chapter 3

It was the end of the line, Rachel thought, it really was the end of the line. The train had slowed as it approached the station and they had slowly and sedately cruised through a wilderness of reclaimed industrial sites and rows of terraced houses, straggling in higgledy piggedly fashion up the sides of the valley.

Wales to her was a place that she'd had some dreary, wet, childhood holidays in. In a place called Rhyl; a town that wore its despair, instead of its heart, on its sleeve. She'd never been to the south of the country and had only vaguely heard of Abermannan, though she couldn't remember exactly when or why she had come across the place.

Everyone on the train got out and either headed for the exit gates or made their way to the other platforms for trains further west. The big 125 was idling, for all the world as if it was panting after its long journey, all the doors were flung open and cleaners – or as they were now called 'train presentation operatives', as if the corporate title could somehow make a menial job more appealing – were rushing onboard with plastic bags and rolls of wipes.

There was no-one manning the gates; they were all locked open. It was as if the train company had no further interest in them. The passengers had chosen to come to Abermannan and it was on their own heads. Rachel had been hoping to find a member of staff to ask directions; Andrews had told her that the police station was in the centre of town and in walking distance of the station. She knew that she could have looked it up on her phone, along with every conceivable mode of transport for getting to the place, but she preferred the personal touch, face-to-face communication. In the end she got a convoluted set of instructions from a young girl working in the cafe on the station concourse – another one of those ubiquitous chains. With a strange mixture of indolence and insolence – well, as Rachel wasn't a customer, she could be as rude she liked – the girl put her on the right road.

Rachel had arrived later than she had intended; she'd made the mistake of going into the office first, not a good move as there was always something to catch up with or something new cropping up. By the time she left Paddington, it was after one o'clock and then there had been a twenty-minute delay around Reading. So, she strode out from the station in a hurry, not sure what sort of office hours these people in the provinces kept.

The police station was a modern purpose-built place, all concrete and glass, standing just up the street from its predecessor, a much more serene and sedate Victorian building. The old station was now part of a college, or so the sign outside said, though it had preserved the cornice above the entrance, carved with the words 'Police Station' and surmounted by an ancient blue lantern. The modern building, in contrast, looked like a fortress; a place of blank walls and slit windows, as if the Abermannan constabulary were expecting to stand off a siege from rioting townspeople.

The desk sergeant – a middle-aged man, running to fat – eyed her up as she walked in and asked, rather curtly:

"Can I help you?"

"I'm looking for Inspector James," she said.

That was all she had. The name. Inspector James. Not Detective Inspector James or Chief Inspector James. No indication of department or division. Nothing else and no appointment either.

"Shall I phone ahead?" She'd asked Anderson on the phone the night before. "Make arrangements?"

"James doesn't work that way," Andrews had answered. "Just go down and see him."

So, Rachel was left with only a vague idea of who she was seeing and why she was seeing him.

"I can't help you, love," the sergeant said, looking rather pleased that he couldn't accommodate her. "He doesn't work here."

Rather irritated by now, Rachel produced her warrant card.

"You should have told me earlier, Sarge, that you were in the job," the desk sergeant said, all chummy now. She was one of them, one of the club.

"Inspector James works out of an annex. His office is in the old Abermannan Hospital at the other end of town."

"Can you call me a taxi?" Rachel asked, by now rather disgruntled with the whole trip.

"I can do better than that. I can give you a lift!"

In fact, it wasn't the sergeant who gave her a lift, but a couple of uniformed officers who were heading down that part of town to give a crime prevention talk. They were friendly enough and quite informal, introducing themselves as Dai and Jackie, but she could see that they were rather intrigued by her presence. After all, it wasn't every day that a detective sergeant from the Met turned up in Abermannan and asked to see Inspector James.

The journey took all of ten minutes, so the conversation was short and perfunctory, though Jackie, as she climbed out of the car and stepped onto the curb to point out the building that Rachel was heading for, smiled at her and said:

"Inspector James is a bit.... how can I put it .... eccentric. So be prepared!"

With that the police car sped away and Rachel was left wondering what she had got herself into.

As it was, she wouldn't have missed the building. The old hospital came from an era when such infirmaries were built in the centre of towns, not on their outskirts, when everyone walked to work and few people, apart from the rich, had cars. It was another of those once-impressive Victorian buildings that the town had grown out of.

There was a reception desk of sorts, though the place looked as desolate and derelict on the inside as it did on the outside. The woman behind the desk was a rather severe-looking middle-aged woman, who looked at Rachel over her reading glasses with something approaching disdain. She asked Rachel if she could help her in tones that suggested that, in fact, she didn't really want to.

"I'm here to see Inspector James," Rachel said, hoping she was in the right place, as the cavernous entrance hall of the old hospital and the anonymous corridors that led off it, didn't look like any police station she had ever been in.

"Please take a seat in the waiting room," the woman said, indicating a door to a glassed-in section of the lobby.

That was all she said. She didn't take Rachel's name, or ask her business, just told her to take a seat. The waiting room was empty. The light outside the hospital was fading and she could see the sick, sodium glare of the street lights coming on. Suddenly Rachel felt exhausted. She hadn't slept that well after Andrews' phone call the night before. The mysterious body and the scene in the club had been going through her head, turning and churning around in her mind. When she did finally get to sleep, she could see that dead face looking at her, the ivory skin and sharp-cut features, and eyes the green of the sea staring at her in her dreams.

She checked her phone and saw that the battery was low, but she couldn't see a power point to plug her charger in and couldn't be bothered to ask the dragon lady on reception. So, instead, to divert herself she flicked through the magazines on the table in front of her. They were mostly what used to be called 'women's magazines' and seemed to be years out of date, all beauty and fashion tips for looks that had become outmoded decades ago. There were also recipes for foods that people no longer ate, a forlorn archaeology of yesterday's lives.

Just as she was getting absorbed in a recipe for a tuna casserole that was mainly canned mushroom soup, the door of the waiting room swung open and a young woman – South Asian, Rachel thought making a quick assessment, Muslim, wearing a hijab – said:

"Detective Sergeant Stevens!"

"That's me," Rachel answered, though she hadn't actually told anyone here her name.

"Inspector James is running late," she smiled as she said this, "well, of course, he always is, but he knows you're waiting. Can I get you a coffee or something?"

"Coffee would be nice," Rachel replied. She needed something to keep her awake, sitting there in the waiting room, the heat from the old cast iron radiators making the atmosphere soporific.

The young woman came back in a few minutes with a cup of coffee and a plate of biscuits.

"Sorry," she said. "No chocolates ones! Phyllis always eats all the chocolate ones!" She nodded her head towards the receptionist.

Rachel thought that Phyllis could probably do with cutting out the chocolate biscuits as she seemed to have overflowed from her chair and onto the desk in front of her.

"My name is Rajma, by the way." The young woman said. "Rajma Ali. I work sometimes with Inspector James."

"Are you in the force?" Rachel asked, because Rajma didn't look like she was a police officer. The police were like the masons; they had a way of acting and talking to one of their own. It was a subtle thing, not a special handshake or anything, just a number of different, easily missable cues.

Rajma laughed at the suggestion.

"No nothing like that," she said. "I'm a sort of consultant."

She smiled as she said it. As if it wasn't at all a serious proposition.

There was a sudden flourish of activity in the hall-way. Two figures had burst through the outside doors and into the lobby. They were deep in conversation and it sounded heated. One of the men was extraordinary enough for Rachel's eyes to be immediately drawn to him. He was big, both tall and wide, probably over six and a half foot. He had on a short, black jacket – a sort of donkey jacket – and he was one of the hairiest men that Rachel had ever seen. He had long black hair - jet black - a full beard and hairs seemed to protrude at his neck and between his wrists and the sleeves of the jacket, which were a bit too short for him. His voice was loud and booming, but she couldn't catch any of his words. She wondered if he was actually speaking English. Perhaps it was Welsh, she thought.

The other man was a much smaller man – perhaps not as small as he appeared, because he was dwarfed by the other man – in a grey top-coat, which seemed to complement his grey hair and beard. He carried a walking stick, but seemed to move easily in small, compact movements, as if he was light on his feet. He seemed to be trying to reason with the bigger man, to calm him down. They abruptly disappeared down one of the corridors, without a word to the receptionist, who seemed disgruntled by the snub.

"There's Inspector James," Rajma said, "he should be with you now."

Now, in this part of the world Rachel found out, didn't mean immediately. She was relieved when she eventually saw the big, hairy man retrace his steps down the corridor and barge out of the front door. She presumed this meant that the smaller man was Inspector James, which was a relief, because though Rachel was not easily intimidated, the big, hairy man seemed quite formidable.

By this time Rajma had disappeared down one of the corridors and the receptionist had packed up – making quite a job of it, opening and closing her handbag several times, collecting things from her drawers and putting other things back, then changing her mind – eventually leaving without a backward glance at Rachel.

It can't be long now, Rachel thought, but then she saw the smaller man scurrying down the corridor and out of the front door, before she had time to intercept him. It was getting late and she was wondering whether she would actually get to see the fabled Inspector James. She was, in fact, just on the point of leaving, wondering whether she could find a hotel with a vacancy somewhere on the promenade, looking down into her bag to check that she hadn't forgotten her toothbrush, when suddenly the man re-appeared in front of her.

"Detective Sergeant Stevens, I presume," he said, with what could only be described as a twinkle in his eye.

Chapter 4

Rachel didn't know that pubs like that still existed anymore. Inspector James - because it really was him - had escorted her out of the building and across the road and then down a side street to a bar called the Beach Hotel, which looked like it was last refurbished before the Second World War. The landlady looked as if she remembered that war and should have retired about twenty years ago. The drinkers were predominantly elderly and, though not particularly friendly, they did acknowledge them when they entered.

The Inspector had apologised on their walk over for keeping her waiting so long.

"I had a bit of a situation," he said. "You probably saw my visitor."

She nodded her agreement.

"Caradog of the Dragon clan," the Inspector said, "he had some grievance with the Black Mountain people. And I didn't want it degenerating into an all-out war. So, I had to broker a peace."

Inspector James confused Rachel. He did not seem to act like a policeman and he had an old-fashioned charm and gallantry that seemed out of place in this day and age, holding doors open for her and pulling out a seat from the table in the pub, so that she could sit down. It was starting to get on her nerves. But his words were even more confusing. What was he on about? She asked herself.

"So, these dragon and mountain people," she asked, "are they travellers?"

"Yes, you could say that," Inspector James replied somewhat archly. "That's a good description."

And then Rachel, just to make conversation, had added an anecdote about her time on the force in Oxfordshire and the pitched battles the travellers had fought in Abingdon over a jilted bride.

"Yes, a similar thing," Inspector James replied, but his attention was elsewhere. He stood up to go to the bar.

"What can I get you to drink?" Inspector James asked.

When they were both sitting in front of their gin and tonics, she got her tablet out of her bag and showed him the pictures of the mysterious corpse.

"It's what I expected," he said, when she had scrolled through all the images, "DCI Andrew told me a lot on the phone."

"So, you've seen this before?" Rachel asked, slightly bemused. The Inspector didn't seem at all taken aback, instead he took it all in his stride.

"Yes," he replied. "But what really concerns me is your little massacre. I'm afraid it might not augur well. It could in fact be the start of something."

The Inspector seemed cagey and he talked in such a guarded matter that he didn't actually appear to be saying anything. Rachel was too tired to deal with it all. If she'd thought that she was going to get some answers, it seemed that she was about to be sorely disappointed.

Inspector James sighed and suddenly said:

"D.I. Stevens, there are probably a few things that I should explain to you, but I can see that you are tired and you must be hungry, so let's go and get something to eat."

It was quite a good curry, even by London standards. Rachel had realised as she sat down that she was in fact hungry, so she'd probably eaten more than she needed to. The nature of her job meant that she went for long periods without really eating anything, discounting the crappy snacks, and then pigged out on something, usually fast, junky food. Ellen was always going on about it to her, because Ellen was good at food and eating. She could not only cook, but would always prepare something healthy for her lunch, which she would take in a sandwich box and eat in the staff room. Rachel had experimented once or twice and taken in a salad, but then she'd either lost the box or left the salad in the fridge too long until it was starting to decompose. So she stuck to her unhealthy eating.

"Would you like another drink?" Inspector James asked as they sat there with the forlorn remnants of the meal spread before them. Rachel had drunk a pint of Kingfisher – well she was thirsty and, technically, they were no longer on duty –but the Inspector had taken water, saying that he was driving.

"No thanks. I should really sort out somewhere to stay," Rachel replied.

"That's not necessary," the Inspector said. "You are quite welcome to stay with me."

The offer made Rachel feel rather uncomfortable. If wasn't that she thought the Inspector had designs on her or her body - she was sure anyway that she could handle herself, sexual harassment had been a fact of life on the force when she had first joined - it was just that she didn't really want the kind of intimacy that staying in someone's house invited. In short, she really didn't want to make friends with him or anyone else, she was down here on a job and it was that simple.

"I couldn't impose," she said. "Not on you or your family."

"It really would be no imposition," he replied, "and I live on my own. There's plenty of room there, so you really wouldn't be in the way."

In the end she agreed, because, after all, it was easier and they still had plenty to talk about. It had almost seemed as if he was avoiding the issue over dinner, either through that politeness of his – no shop talk at the table – or because he was prevaricating.

Getting into a rather non-descript old Ford, Rachel was rather disappointed that Inspector James didn't have a little vintage sports car or some other unusual vehicle to go with his rather eccentric manner and way of dressing. Because he was different and she might have, if she was being uncharitable, have called him a weirdo. He wore a grey three-piece tweed suit, with a matching grey topcoat and leather gloves. There was no hint of a mobile phone or a digital watch, but he had an old, gold repeater that he wore in the pocket of his waistcoat on a watch chain, and he checked this once or twice in the course of the evening. He still affected the walking stick, though she didn't think that he had any difficulty walking.

More than the dress, it was his manner that was different. He was scrupulously polite, not only in his mannerisms and the little flourishes that he demonstrated, the opening of doors and pulling out of chairs which she had already noticed, but also in the rather avuncular way in which he sat and listened and seemed intent on her every word. His voice was cultured and educated, but with a marked local accent – posh Welsh as she remembered someone had called it – and he was very soft-spoken, not at all hearty or boisterous. So different from most of the policemen of that rank and age that she had previously known. But then she wondered was he actually a policeman, because what did she truly know about him.

As he started driving, she again thought of how little she knew the man and it made her wonder whether she was, in fact, being foolish, going back to his house. But as he pulled out onto the coast road and she saw the lights of the promenade and a full moon over Abermannan Bay flooding light onto the sands, she started to relax a little. By the time he pulled up in front of the house, she'd put her worries behind her. It was a fascinating old building, built on a hill just above the village at the end of the bay, with a large garden and spectacular views of the arc of sea and land below.

Picking up on her interest, the Inspector said:

"It's an Edwardian villa built about 1910. By that time the village had become a seaside resort and people were building holiday homes or hotels for the summer visitors."

The Inspector insisted on carrying her hold-all in from the car. Though it was light, Rachel felt rather guilty about this. The house had a porch and a stained-glass window light above the door. The front door opened into a hallway, bigger than some hotel lobbies Rachel had been in, with a wide stairway climbing to the first and second floors. Inside it was all wood panelling, wooden floors and old, frayed carpets. It wasn't old-fashioned exactly, just timeless.

"I'll show you to your room," Inspector James said and led her up the stairs.

It wasn't an enormous house, Rachel noted, but the rooms were airy and high, giving that illusion of space. She thought there were about four or five bedrooms upstairs, going on the doors that led off the landing. He led her into a bedroom that looked out over the rocky point at the end of the bay and the lighthouse beyond.

"I hope you'll be comfortable here," he said. "The bathroom is along the hall, so feel free to shower or freshen up. There are towels in the airing cupboard in the bathroom. Perhaps you would like to join me downstairs when you are ready and we can talk about your case."

Though Rachel did feel rather uncomfortable creeping around a strange house, she did take a shower – it had been a long day – with the result that she felt somewhat refreshed when she descended the stairs and found the drawing room where the Inspector was sitting. There were two wing-backed chairs in front of an open fire and a bottle of wine and two glasses on a small table between the chairs. Both the warmth and the wine were welcome.

The Inspector poured Rachel a glass of wine and then sat back down.

"You must have questions, D.S. Stevens so please feel free to ask them."

Rachel took a sip of the wine and stared into the fire. It was true she did have questions, the main ones being why had she come to this town and was she actually wasting her time.

"I don't know why I'm here, Sir," she said.

"You don't have to call me, Sir," the Inspector replied, "unless you really want to."

He smiled at her and went on:

"D.I. Andrews probably didn't want to tell you too much. He probably didn't want to put you off."

"Sorry, Inspector, I'm not following you," Rachel said. She had to call him something, so if not 'Sir' then it would have to be 'Inspector'.

"Andrews sent you here because we have a particular expertise in handling the sort of case – the two cases I should say – that you are involved with."

Curiouser and curiouser, Rachel thought, echoing Alice.

"In short," Inspector James went on, "I run a special unit that deals with certain types of crimes that police forces find difficult to cope with."

Rachel's face must have betrayed her consternation because James quickly added:

"I think that you already know, Rachel, that you are not dealing with ordinary crimes here. I hope you don't mind if I call you Rachel, by the way, D.S. Stevens seems too formal."

At that moment, Rachel didn't actually care what he called her.

"What do you mean, Inspector?"

"The pictures of the corpse you showed me, of the course. What is your explanation for its strange appearance?"

Rachel thought a moment before she answered.

"The pathologist thought the body was East European or Slavic with a surgical modification to the ears, possibly cosmetic."

Her answer sounded trite, even to her.

"But what do you think, Rachel?"

"Well, there was no scarring around the ears, so it could be a birth anomaly, couldn't it?"

"What other explanation could there be?" She might have felt that Inspector James was interrogating her, but he that twinkle in his eye, an inherent amusement that made it more of a parlour game than an inquisition.

Rachel laughed.

"You're not suggesting that we are dealing with elves, are you?" She asked. Though, in truth, the implications of what he was saying were starting to make her feel uncomfortable.

"No, Rachel, elves are fictional creations. And J.R.R. Tolkien has a lot to answer for, in my opinion. I'm not talking about elves."

Inspector James stood up and refilled her glass, she had not noticed that she had effectively drained it. It was a nervous habit of hers, downing drinks when she was stressed, and, over the years, it had got her into all kinds of trouble.

The Inspector sat down again.

"No, Rachel, I'm talking about the Tylwyth Teg."

"Is that some sort of criminal gang?" Rachel asked, thinking that it might be a Welsh version of the Triads or the Mafia.

"Tylwyth Teg translates as Fair Folk, also known as the Bendith y Mamau, the blessing of the mothers, and Gwyllion, or creatures of the dark, though the latter term doesn't really translate very well into English."

"I don't understand," Rachel said.

"I'm taking about fairies!" The Inspector answered.

"Fairies?" Rachel exclaimed and all she could think of was Tinkerbelle, with her gossamer wings and her butterfly brain. "Supernatural creatures?"

"Or if you put it another way," James said. "The vestige of the original indigenous population of these isles. Creatures who retreated from human beings and human society as we tamed the wilderness that they haunted. Creatures that never went away, who are always there and seldom come into contact with humans."

The Inspector looked at her and asked:

"What do you think?"

"I don't know what to think," Rachel said.

"Then let's leave supposition aside for the moment and you tell me about the rings and the other jewelry that you mentioned your corpse was wearing."

She showed Inspector James the pictures of the rings and the pendant on her tablet.

"Interesting," he said, "your fellow was quite a way from home. If I'm not mistaken he comes from one of the domains in the north west of England. Cumbria, I think."

"You can tell that from these?" Rachel asked.

"Designs and markings are associated with different domains or kingdoms. The Fair Folk themselves are not one homogenous people; they have their divisions, their rivalries and their conflicts."

He handed her back the tablet.

"And you say the body was taken?"

"Yes," Rachel answered. "Stolen from the morgue."

"They wouldn't leave their dead in human hands. It was an odd fact in itself that he was found alone, away from any companions. As the Fair Folk are not lone or solitary creatures."

"But he was dressed in modern clothes; a suit, hand-made shoes."

The Inspector smiled.

"They may keep away from humans, but they are quite conscious of our ways and customs. If one of them chooses to move amongst us, he or she will disguise themselves as best they can to fit in."

Rachel shook her head, it must all too much and she was tired. Perhaps it was all a hallucination, she thought. Maybe the curry had hallucinogenic qualities.

"What we have to find out, Rachel," the Inspector said, "is why and how the Fair Folk have come into contact and conflict with these people in London. From what Andrews told me, the men who were killed or injured in that club were part of a gang, so some of their activities must have brought them into conflict with this particular band of Fair Folk."

The Inspector glanced over at Rachel and smiled again, a look of sympathy rather than amusement

"A lot to take in, I know. So perhaps you should sleep on it and we can talk in the morning."

Chapter 5

Rachel didn't usually have difficulty sleeping in a strange place – there had been so many over the years – but her sleep was disturbed by a dream again, a vivid one, where the corpse from the morgue came alive and pursued her, then suddenly pulled a mask off and revealed itself as Inspector James.

She woke abruptly from this dream and checked her phone; it was nearly 4am. Usually she would have rolled over and tried to drift off again, as she tended to be a good sleeper, but her bladder was telling her that she needed a pee. It was the beer, she thought, it always happened when she drank beer. In her drowsy state, she had to make a conscious effort to remember where she was, to sit up and swing her legs over the side of the bed, and, before venturing out of the room, try to recall where the bathroom was located.

As it was, she missed the correct door and went off wandering down the hallway, until she emerged on the landing, knowing then that she had gone too far. But before she retraced her steps, she paused. Above the stairs as it climbed from the ground floor to the top floor of the building was a wide, deep, stained glass window, the sort of thing you saw in buildings of this age, and the light of the moon shining through the glass was throwing a kaleidoscopic pattern of colour and shadow over the landing and the stairs.

She stood there for a few seconds just taking in the wonder of the scene, but then she was conscious of the slightest of sounds coming from the landing above her, where the attic rooms were and the tall, obscure figure of a woman, in some sort of diaphanous robe, started to slowly descend the stairs. She couldn't really see the woman clearly; the light was too diffuse and the pattern of shadow too confusing to the eye. All she saw was a slim, elegant form, slowly moving from step to step, pausing often. And as she moved the woman was humming or singing something to herself.

Rachel quickly slunk back into the hallway, found the bathroom, had a pee and then went back to her room. She felt like she had intruded; after all this was the woman's house and she was the stranger. But before sleep overtook her again, she remembered something that Inspector James had said. He had told her that he lived alone.

Morning came and found her still sleeping. She cursed herself when she looked at her phone and saw the time. It was after 8am. She had meant to get up earlier. She wondered if Inspector James would think her terribly unprofessional, sleeping through her alarm like that. She didn't shower, just sluiced her face, quickly brushed her hair and tumbled down the stairs towards the kitchen, from where she could hear the noise of dishes clinking and the calm, measured tones of a radio announcer.

There was something about waking up at the sea-side, she thought. The light from the sea was illuminating the stained-glass window, a different more subtle glow than last night, and there was a warm breeze blowing from somewhere, a tang of salt in the air.

To her surprise, when she walked into the kitchen, it was Rajma who greeted her, not Inspector James.

"Morning Rachel," she said, as if they were old friends.

Rachel mumbled a response; she wasn't good in the mornings. Rajma offered her coffee and something to eat.

"Just coffee, please," Rachel said, though she could hear a chorus of voices in her head – a duet, her mother and Ellen – whispering that breakfast was the most important meal of the day.

"You are probably wondering where Inspector James is," Rajma said, pre-empting the question that Rachel's foggy mind was formulating.

"Something came up this morning. An emergency. He sends his apologies and has asked me to drive you to the station."

"Oh," Rachel said, wide awake now. "I was hoping to talk some more to him this morning."

Rajma smiled.

"Inspector James always seems to be dashing off at short notice, I'm afraid. He did also ask me to tell you that he will come to you in London in two days."

"Did he give a time or suggest a place?" Rachel asked. She hated waiting around for people and, besides, vague arrangements like this irritated her.

"Oh! Don't worry about that!" Rajma said. "He'll find you!"

After Rachel had finished her coffee, there was nothing left to delay them further. They climbed into Rajma's little Citroen and set off.

"We should make the ten o'clock train," Rajma said. "So, you'll be back in London by lunchtime."

Rachel glanced back as they drove through the gates at the end of the drive, it might have been the light, but she was almost sure she saw a face at one the first-floor windows.

Rajma drove along the coast road, quite empty at this time of the day and they kept up a desultory conversation, the sort that people do have in cars.

"So, Rajma, were you ever on the force?" Rachel asked. "Before you became a consultant, that is."

"No, my background is in anthropology. I was an academic before I came to work for the unit."

"Inspector James didn't say that much about the unit yesterday." Rachel said. "He didn't have much of a chance. It's part of the South Wales police force isn't it?"

"Not exactly," Rajma said. "It's more of an independent organisation."

Rachel was experienced enough in interrogating suspects to know that Rajma was being guarded, if not actually disingenuous.

"To be honest," Rajma continued. "I don't really know how the unit fits in with the wider picture. Inspector James handles all of that."

They had left the coast road by now and Rajma was negotiating the town traffic.

"So, do you deal with fairies, too?" Rachel asked, watching Rajma's face for a reaction. She had deliberately asked the question in a flippant way, trying to get the woman to react. But Rajma didn't take the bait.

"No," she answered, quite coolly, "that's Inspector James' area, amongst other things. I deal with other phenomena."

Rachel couldn't get over the matter-of-fact way in which these people talked of such things. It would seem laughable, ludicrous, if it wasn't for that body on the slab. And, though it was gone, she hadn't imagined it; she had the pictures to prove it.

"What do you do then?" Rachel asked, genuinely interested now.

"Oh, I deal with Djinns," Rajma answered, smiling at Rachel. They were in the station car park now and she'd parked the car.

"Djinns!" Rachel said. "You mean genies!"

"It's a long story, Rachel," Rajma said. "I'll tell you all about it one day, when we have more time." She looked at her watch. "But we should hurry or you'll miss your train!"

The London train was waiting. It was a big 125, with plenty of room for Rachel to find a seat on her own away from other people. Rajma walked her to the platform and Rachel climbed up the steps into the train. The guard checked the doors and then blew his whistle. Rachel opened the window.

"Thanks for the lift, Rajma," she said.

"You're welcome! Have a safe journey!"

"Perhaps we'll meet again?"

"Oh, I'm sure we will!"

Rajma was just turning to go, when she hesitated.

"I know you find this all difficult to believe, Rachel. I did once."

Rachel didn't know how to answer the woman, but then something occurred to her, just as the train was starting to pull out.

"There was a woman in the house last night, when I got up to look for the bathroom. Do you know who she was?"

Rajma looked quizzical.

"The Inspector lives on his own, Rachel," she replied.

Then the train rolled out of Abermannan.

Chapter 6

Rachel spent the first hour of her journey going over the events of the last twenty-four hours in her head. It all could have been some strange hallucination, hours out of time, out of her life, a fantasy or a dream. But then she came back to the body on the morgue slab, the killings in the club and she knew that she couldn't discount what Inspector James had told her. There was something strange in all this, something other, but she just couldn't believe that it was all down to these so-called fairies. There must be another explanation.

Her reverie was interrupted by her phone, just after they'd stopped at Cardiff. It was Andrews.

"How's it going down there?" He asked.

"I'm on the way back," she replied.

"Really, so soon?" Andrews sounded disappointed. "Anything come out of it? Any leads?"

"To be honest, Sir," Rachel replied. "I'm more confused than ever. How much do you actually know about Inspector James and his unit?"

There was a pause on the other end of the phone, and then Andrews said.

"I think we need to talk about that in person. Besides, there have been some more developments."

From the outside, the house looked like any of the others on the street. This was a typical street in a typical suburb of London. The houses were sizeable, semi-detached dwellings built in the 1920s or 1930s for the lower middle classes and they still maintained the look of shabby gentility. Rachel didn't know Southgate that well. It didn't really feel like London to her. It was outside the Northern Circular road and was one of those orbital districts that seemed like a sort of no-man's-land between the city and the surrounding countryside. Garibaldi Street was as anonymous as any other street in any other similar district.

On closer inspection, though, number twenty-one was different from its neighbours. For a start it had been extensively modernised, expensively if not tastefully. Someone had thought it a good idea to give a touch of the mock Georgians to the front of the house, adding a portico and pillars.

"Airs and graces!" Andrews said, as they pulled up in the car. "A bargain basement Downton Abbey!"

The portico jarred with the mundane, homely architecture of the rest of the place. The fence didn't do the house any favours, either. While the other neighbours all had low walls and open driveways, the front garden of twenty one was enclosed by a palisade of ornamental railings, the entrance sealed by gates, with security lights and cameras at all the angles. It was obvious to everyone - was, in fact, on display for everyone to see - that the inhabitants of the house were well-off and that money, Rachel knew, hadn't come from honest labour or hard toil. Because this was the house of Tony Francis and he was a scion of the Francis family.

If the Francis family had had a family motto, it would have been something like:

"Proudly robbing the local community for three generations; bringing crime and mayhem to a street near yours."

Old Granddad Bert Francis and his wife Doris - scarier than the old man, if what the old-time coppers said was true – were relative small fry. Just local villains. He ran a scrap yard – at least that was his one legitimate business – and did a sideline in nicked roof lead and copper wire and pipes. He also did some thuggery on the side and that's how his two sons got into the business, branching out into loan sharking and protection money. Dave and Robbie were a sort of diet version of the Krays – or should that be a low-fat version, Rachel thought, as they were both skinny runts - never as dangerous or notorious, definitely in their shadow, but owing a lot to the twins in terms of style and viciousness.

The Francis family's fortunes had really improved with the arrival of smack on the North London Estates in the last quarter of the twentieth century. By that time Bert was dead and Doris was in a home, suffering from dementia. They'd gone from a small firm of thugs and bully boys to a major drugs gang. The thing about heroin, then cocaine and then crack, was that there was so much money in it, so much pure profit. And now Andy, grandson of Bert, was rolling in it. On the surface he was a legitimate business man, with a portfolio of clubs and restaurants and the like. He was even a major donor to the Tory party, but every policeman and every criminal in North London knew where the money really came from.

Andy's father Dave had retired to the Costa del Sol years ago and his uncle Robbie had had his head blown off by a sawn-off shotgun at close range in a drug deal gone wrong at the end of the nineties. So, Andy was the kingpin now. But Tony wasn't actually a Francis, though he had adopted the name; his real surname was Wilson. He was small fry, no more than a driver and a gopher, unimportant really, it would appear, except for one minor detail. He was Tony's brother-in-law, married to Deb, Andy's younger sister. And Andy doted on Deb, he always had.

And now Rachel and her boss had the dubious privilege of having been summoned by a member of the Francis family, a clan who were not known for their dealings with the police, unless you counted the odd bent copper. It was Deb who had phoned 999.

Andrews talked into the entry phone and had a brief conversation with a disembodied voice. The gate slid open with a smooth oiled action – obviously the best that money could buy, Rachel thought. It was Deb herself who opened the double front door and ushered them into the lounge. She had that perma-tanned complexion that spoke of money and leisure, gold rings on her fingers and a gold necklace. Rachel didn't know much about haute couture, but the dress that Deb was wearing looked expensive – it was a tawny silk number – and fell nicely over her gym-toned body.

"Your lot have already been," she said to Andrews. Her voice and vocabulary were still North London, though it was overlaid with a more neutral accent. Deb was doing her best to speak posh, Rachel thought. "They told me I should wait before reporting it."

"I'm D.I. Andrews, as I told you," Andrews said. "And this is D.S. Stevens. You reported your husband missing, so it becomes a matter for the detective branch."

This wasn't exactly true, as they both knew. You only treated someone as missing if they had been gone for 24 hours and then you investigated, but in this case the Francis family were involved, which meant there could be serious consequences. If someone had abducted a Francis, the firm would want payback.

"You told our officers that you came home from lunch and Tony wasn't here."

Rachel thought that it figured that Deb was a lady who lunched, a member of that semi-mythical tribe that she'd never encountered before. Most of the women she knew didn't have the time, the money, or the inclination to do so.

"Why was that a concern, Deborah?" Andrews continued. "You don't mind if I call you Deborah, by the way, it sounds less formal than Mrs. Francis?"

Deb smiled and fluttered her eyelashes. Andrews was turning on the charm and she had fallen for it. It was that soft Borders accent that his voice had, Rachel decided, like female Viagra.

"Tony is a creature of habit, Mr. Andrews," Deb said. "He was off work today, feeling a bit unwell, and he said that he was going to stay in and watch a DVD. He wouldn't have changed his plans without telling me."

"Please call me Donald," Andrews said, and Deb batted her eyelids again, that secret little smile on her face still. "Now can you tell me if there was anything unusual about the house when you got back? Was there a sign of a struggle, for instance?"

"No, nothing like that, Donald," Deb said, using the name tentatively, as if she shouldn't really, "but the gate and the front door were wide open."

"I see," Andrews said. "Now I think you have CCTV, Deborah. Is that correct?"

She nodded. Her face looked like a light bulb had suddenly been switched on in her head. She obviously hadn't thought of this.

"Yes," she said. "We can play it back from Tony's computer, in his study."

The study was a long, low room, part of the extension which had been brutally pushed out into a once-sizeable back garden. Deb and her husband had tried to turn a North London family home into a mansion and, like a slim-fit shirt on a fat man, it didn't sit that well. It was all bulges and odd protuberances where you least expected.

Rachel figured that Tony did very little studying in his study. It was in fact more a games room or a male den, with a full-size billiard table, a home cinema system with a row of authentic cinema chairs and a well-stocked bar fitted into the angle of one of the walls. There was also, however, an expensive personal computer on what looked to be an antique walnut desk – though it was probably a modern copy. The PC looked as if it had been bought more for form than function and the desk around it was scrupulously tidy – no stray papers or bills or loose pens – suggesting that it was little used.

Deb, however, knew exactly what she was doing and had soon opened the relevant files.

"Tony doesn't really understand computers," she said almost apologetically, "so I'm the one who has to sort this stuff."

The stuff in question was a number of digital video recordings from the CCTV cameras. Deb was just trying to sort through them, getting rather flustered, when the entry phone buzzed.

"Excuse me," she said. "I'll be back in a sec."

And she was. But she wasn't alone. She'd brought her brother Andy along with her.

Rachel had never met Andy Francis before, but she knew him by sight; she'd seen enough pictures of him, in files and newspapers, and there was plenty of TV footage of him being interviewed on the steps of various crown courts. He looked better in the flesh – TV added about half a stone – but he still looked like a rather smug, middle-aged business man.

He had rather let himself go – too many business lunches and corporate dinners – and was carrying a bit of weight, especially around the belly, but he still looked powerful enough, with a casual air of brutality that hung around him like a rather unpleasant after-shave, however much he tried to mask it with expensive suits and cashmere coats. Like Deb, he was perm-tanned and shared a predilection for gold against the yellow-brown of his skin; rings, a gold Rolex, gold chain around his neck. His hair looked too blonde, too bleached for a man of his age, forty going on fifty, but nobody was going to tell him that.

Today, he looked as if he had just come from the golf course, wearing the sort of check trousers that only a golfer could get away with and some sort of bright Lycra top. Perhaps the game had not gone as well as he hoped, Rachel thought, because he didn't look happy. Though he adopted a studied politeness with Andrews, there was an underlying tone of menace in his voice.

"Deb told me you were here, D.I. Andrews," he said, ignoring Rachel almost completely, just giving her the odd sidelong glance. "I'm afraid there's been a bit of a mix-up."

It transpired, or so Andy said, that Tony wasn't missing after all.

"He had to run an errand for me, a business matter, at short notice. He should have texted Deb, but he's a bit of a duffer with all this new technology." Andy said, a smile on his face. "We're terribly sorry to have troubled you for nothing."

As Andy ushered them out – getting them away from the CCTV files as quickly as possible – Rachel glanced at Deb's face and saw, all in a moment, that she wasn't convinced by the story.

And neither were Andrews and Rachel. They sat in the car across the road from the house, the gates and the door of the place now firmly closed to them.

"What do you make of that?" Andrews asked.

"I'd say that somebody's got Tony, Boss." Rachel answered.

"I wish we had got a look at that CCTV footage," Andrews said.

"We'll just have to do it the old-fashioned way," Rachel said, looking out of the car window at the house opposite twenty one.

Mrs. Levy served them tea and cakes within ten minutes of answering her front door. Rachel had prepared a story – about how they were investigating a string of burglaries in the area – but it was completely unnecessary. Mrs. Levy was always willing to help the police, she said, and ushered them in without even checking their warrant cards.

The old lady had a pair of pug dogs, the sort that seem to be constantly asthmatic. Rachel was not a dog person at the best of times - a fact she put down to having a Caribbean mother – and she thought that the doleful expressions and squashed-in faces of the small dogs, which made them look suicidally depressed, were not at all softened by their rather yappy and ill-tempered dispositions. Andrews, however, played up to them, which seemed to please Mrs. Levy, and, in no time at all, she was treating him like an old friend. Rachel wondered, wryly, why she was so immune to Andrews' charm, whereas Deb and the old lady were so taken with him.

Mrs. Levy told them in no uncertain terms that she wasn't a busybody and didn't believe in being a nosey neighbour, but she said, qualifying her statement, you couldn't sometimes help noticing things, especially odd or unusual things. And that morning she had noticed something that she thought was strange. She'd seen a van parked outside number twenty one – no, she hadn't seen it arrive, when she'd looked out it was already there – and then she'd seen four men carrying something from the house and putting it in the back of the van.

"They were wearing coats and hats. I think they had sunglasses on, which was unusual as it was cloudy. They were carrying a long box."

Andrews asked her what sort of box.

"I don't know, it could have been a coffin. But nobody has died, have they?"

They managed to extricate themselves eventually, thanking Mrs. Levy profusely.

"Well," Andrews said, as they drove away, "either somebody killed Tony or they kidnapped him. And the odd thing is there was no sign of a struggle, no broken doors or forced locks, so Tony must have let them in."

Back at the station in the late afternoon, Rachel tried to piece together what appeared to be the few, disparate pieces of a much bigger jigsaw. The first piece was the body on the slab in the morgue; that of a fairy, if you believed Inspector James. The second piece was the Hav, the site of some sort of fight, which had resulted in a number of deaths and injuries. The only clue that the incidents at the Hav were connected with the body was the nature of the weapons involved; swords and crossbows, not the sort of arms that any self-respecting modern criminal would use. Then there was the abduction, or possible murder of Tony Francis, or Wilson, whatever you wanted to call him.

All the connections and links were quite tenuous. You could surmise certain things, go on a hunch, but there was, in fact, little concrete evidence to go on. She had checked out the ownership of the Hav, but it was some sort of shell company, which couldn't be directly tied to Andy Francis.

She was staring out of her window at a wilderness of suburban back gardens, when her phone rang, startling her.

"D.S. Stevens," a voice said. "I think we have got something – or should I say someone – for you."

It was Harris, the duty officer in the custody suite, over on Caledonian Road.

"But be prepared, you won't have seen anything like this!"

Bur Rachel had seen something like it – like him – on a slab in a morgue. She looked through the two-way mirror into the interview room and noted the similarities. The man – if man he was – was dressed in the same sort of expensive suit and shoes and had all the outward appearance of a businessman or office worker of some sort. That was, of course, if you discounted the pale, waxy skin, the long grey hair and the rather pointed features. Rachel was sure that, somewhere under those flowing locks, were two pointed ears.

"What do you make of him, then?" Harris, standing beside her asked. "Is he a fugitive from some Death Metal band or something?"

Rachel had put a routine call out, after the body had disappeared from the morgue, for traffic to look out for the van that had featured in the CCTV footage. It had been a forlorn hope. The van was a Ford Transit, a bog-standard vehicle, and she had had little hope of anything coming from it. But, incredibly, it had. A couple of PCSOs had called the number in of a van that was parked on a double yellow line in Finsbury Park. There was something wrong with the index number, as the DVLA didn't have it on file, so a car had gone out to investigate and managed to intercept the driver when he came back to it.

The driver was uncooperative – to say the least, as he had tried to leg it – and the two officers had brought him in on suspicion of any offence that they could think up.

"He hasn't said a word," Harris said, "I don't even know if he speaks English. But he's got a very expressive glare. He's obviously not enjoying his stay with us."

Rachel experienced the glare fully, when she interviewed the creature. Andrews hadn't been available – some ACPO committee or something – so Rachel had brought D.C. Thomas with her. He had seemed quite flattered by this and Rachel didn't have the heart to tell him that she just wanted him to make up the numbers.

Rachel started the interview the usual way; advising the suspect of his rights and telling him that he was voluntarily co-operating with the police, but she got no response. The creature – man or whatever he was – just fixed his green eyes on her.

"English? Do you speak any English?" She asked, but the creature made no response.

"Francais? Espanol?" She ran through her limited gamut of languages.

"I think we need an interpreter," Thomas said, rather superfluously.

"Yes. But which language?"

"Is he some sort of East European?" Thomas mused. It seemed to be the standard response to these unfamiliar creatures, as if there was some strange little alien territory, somewhere on the borders of Europe, where people had pointed ears and green eyes.

As Rachel suspected, they got nowhere. The creature just sat silently, not responding to any stimulus. Thomas offered him a cup of tea, going as far as to bring in a cup and mimic drinking, but he was met with a blank stare. It was like having a statue in the room, as if the creature was going into some kind of inner lockdown, going down into the depths and not intending to surface.

They got somewhat further with the creature's personal effects; gold rings, earrings, a pendant, all similar to those that had come from the body in the morgue.

"What do you make of all this, Sarge?" Thomas asked "Have you got any idea what this is all about?"

"No," said Rachel. "I've got my suspicions, but I know a man who might be able to shed some light on the matter."

Chapter 7

By the time Rachel got back to the flat she was exhausted. She could hardly believe it was the same day; that she had left Abermannan that morning. She checked her mail and then had a shower. While she was drying herself, she heard her mobile going off. It was Ellen.

"Are you back yet?" She asked.

Ellen, in her usual efficient way, was just checking if Rachel was there for dinner. They decided to get a take-away, as they were both too tired to cook.

Ellen picked it up from the local Indian – it was on her way back from the tube – and they sat in front of the telly to eat it, their usual practice.

"Shit day?" Ellen asked as she was clearing up. Rachel was at the sink washing the dishes.

"No. Just tired and confusing!"

"You haven't told me how the trip went," Ellen said, sitting at the kitchen table, while Rachel dried the two plates and the cutlery.

"I don't know what to say about it," Rachel said. "That was the confusing part of things."

"How so?" Ellen asked. Rachel could see that Ellen was intrigued, but something - a voice inside her head, you could say – told her that she should be careful what she told the woman, cautious.

"What if all the things that you have taken for granted, all the certainties in your life, are suddenly turned upside down and inside out, by some new knowledge?" Rachel knew that that the question was imprecise and that she wasn't explaining herself well, but she was too tired to think.

"Then, perhaps you need to accept the new reality and learn to live with it," Ellen replied. "Anyway, I'll have to say goodnight. I've got lessons to prepare for tomorrow."

She got up from the table, but then hesitated and said:

"You know where I am, if you need to talk."

It was only when Rachel was lying in bed later that she realised that Ellen had probably taken what she said the wrong way.

"She probably thinks that I just came out to her," Rachel thought.

It wasn't until the next morning that Rachel realised that she had a dilemma. The creature they'd taken into custody – she told herself that she should call it a fairy, but found it difficult to actually mouth the words without feeling ridiculous – would have to be charged or released within twenty four hours. So that meant they had until 5pm that afternoon. She really needed to tell Inspector James and, hopefully, get him to come up to London as soon as possible to interview the fairy – there, she had said it, if only to herself.

The problem was, she had no direct way of contacting the Inspector. She didn't have a direct line to his office and she didn't even know if he had a mobile phone, let alone whether he used one. She grabbed her gym stuff rather grimly and left the house with showering or breakfasting.

She was grim-faced because she knew that she had to go to the gym, though she didn't really want to. She paid a monthly subscription and she was well aware that she was wasting her money if she didn't go at least twice a week and this would be her first visit for ages. So, whether she liked it or not, she was going.

At the gym, before she went on the treadmill, she phoned Abermannan police station to try and get contact details for the Inspector; the desk sergeant couldn't, or wouldn't, help her, but she got him to take a message. When she was showering afterwards, she realised that Andrews must have a way of contacting Inspector James, but when she tried his number when she got back to her car, all she got was his answer phone and, when she tried the station, she was told that he wasn't in his office.

She mulled over the problem on the drive in and later at her desk. There was nothing to charge the fairy with. They had eventually found out from the DVLA that there was a record of the van, so it wasn't stolen, but it was supposed to be off the road, as the owner had a SORN. There seemed to be some question over who actually owned it, but the DVLA were unlikely to get the bottom of things before the twenty four hours were up.

So, she couldn't charge the fairy with theft; it was debatable whether she could get him for driving without a license or driving without insurance as he wasn't actually driving when he was arrested, just sitting in the van. Even if she could throw a negligible charge at him, it would probably be too minor to allow her to hold him. He'd probably get a caution, which he wouldn't understand anyway.

Rachel had enough to do without the distractions of fairy corpses, kidnapped criminals and mute villains. She had a lot of paperwork to wade through, reports to file, and notes to type up from her notebook. Therefore, it was a welcome distraction when Sam – the young woman constable from the Hav – walked in.

"Sarge! Can I have a quick word?" She asked. Rachel motioned for her to sit down.

"Well, it might be nothing," she said, "but I just need to run it past you."

Rachel knew that Sam – otherwise known as Constable Samantha Cunningham, a bundle of clean-limbed and wholesome enthusiasm – was a beat policeman in the neighbourhood around the Hav and had some contact with the women there.

"Well, Sarge, as you know we got nothing out of the working girls at the Hav, they all clammed up."

Rachel nodded her agreement.

"And all their statements have gone to MIT, for whatever their worth," she said.

"Yes, Sarge. But one of the girls told me something the other day, on the QT."

The rather archaic phrase sounded almost quaint coming from the young woman's lips, Rachel thought, and then told herself to stop being so patronising.

"My partner and I were called to a domestic dispute yesterday. It was one of the girls who works at the Hav. A Hungarian called Magda. She's a masseuse there."

"Aren't they all?" Rachel asked.

"Well, that's sort of the point, Sarge," Sam said. "Magda said that there's been a bit more going on there recently. More than the classic massage-and-happy-ending thing."

Rachel poured them coffee, as she thought that this was going to be a long, involved story.

"Basically," Sam went on, "Magda was quite shaken up, so I'd taken her to her bedroom, while my partner had taken her boyfriend outside to the car to calm him down. Magda told me that she was still shaky after what happened at the Hav and she got really upset."

"So where are we going with this?" Rachel asked, she had a terribly short attention span.

"Well, Magda told me that what happened at the Hav was because of what she called the 'other girls'. These were girls brought in and not allowed to mix with the other women. They were moved in after dark and then moved out again in the morning."

"Is that all she could tell you about it?" Rachel asked.

"One of Andy Francis' men told her that they were being taken to a place out of town. They were offering a special service, something very exclusive for clients who were rich, or so it was rumoured."

"Did she say anything else?" Rachel asked.

"All she would say was that the people who raided the Hav were after the other girls. They'd come to take them back."

Chapter 8

Rachel had a late lunch, just a quick sandwich and a coffee. She was feeling frustrated and sorry for herself; the picture, rather than clearing, was getting even more opaque. She had rung Abermannan police station again, a number of times, but, in the end, the desk sergeant had almost put the phone down on her. Andrews was still unreachable and she felt as if she had been left alone to sort out the baffling and inexplicable details of the case.

She nodded to the civilian receptionist on the desk as she walked back into the station and the woman, who was staring at her computer screen – probably watching cat videos, Rachel thought - took a few seconds to react.

"D.S. Stephens," she shouted after Rachel, "you've got a visitor."

"Who is it?" Rachel asked.

"An old man and a child. I told then you were out, but he was very insistent. So, I put him in one of the interview rooms."

The 'old man and child' description and the fact that the Inspector hadn't produced his warrant card – plus the fact that Rachel was distracted by the host of other things that she had to do that afternoon – meant that Rachel was somewhat taken aback when she entered the interview room.

"Oh! It's you, Inspector." She said. She was about to say that she hadn't been expecting him, but, of course, she had been.

"I'm sorry if we've kept you waiting," she added. "If you'd introduced yourself at the front desk. I'm sure they would have found me sooner."

The Inspector smiled at her, rather indulgently, as if she had said something that was interesting but irrelevant.

"It's probably better to keep this visit as informal as we can," he said. "I hear that you have someone in custody."

"Did you get my message?" Rachel asked.

"No," the Inspector answered. "But I do get to know these sorts of things."

The Inspector was either dressed in exactly the same suit and coat she has seen him in two days ago, or he possessed several different sets of them, all uniformly grey and muted. She noted that he had his walking stick and had also accessorised his outfit with a leather briefcase, worn and battered and looking like it dated from the 1940s. But it wasn't so much the Inspector who drew her attention, but the figure with him.

Rachel could see how this person could have been taken for a child. She was quite short – probably not more than five feet tall – and was very slight. Her body looked almost pre-pubescent at first glance, though on closer inspection it was obvious that she was older than she seemed. Her hair was short and mousey-coloured and framed a face that wore a rather vacuous, child-like expression, emphasised and enhanced by small, turned-up nose. Though her face was small and her features were delicate and also belied her age, the wrinkles around her eyes and on her forehead showed her to be older than she appeared at first glance.

The girl's general oddness of appearance was further accentuated by the way she acted when Rachel greeted her. Though she put a limp hand out to be shaken, she cast her eyes down and didn't speak or respond in any way to Rachel's polite greeting.

"Rowena is here to assist us," Inspector James said and Rachel couldn't help wondering, as she drove them over to the Caledonian Road, what sort of assistance the girl was capable of. In her faded jeans and old sweater, a wool coat that had seen better days, and bearing in mind the fact that she seemed totally overwhelmed and almost paralysed by the big city, it was hard to see how much use she could be.

But Rachel was to be proved wrong. When the Inspector introduced Rowena to Harris as an interpreter, she thought he was misleading the man, but she proved to be exactly that. When they were finally sitting across the table from the creature and Inspector James started the interview – after politely seeking Rachel's permission to do so – with Rowena translating his questions, the fairy suddenly lost his composure. He let out a string of angry words – or so Rachel presumed - pushed his chair backwards and stood up.

Rowena then emitted an equally angry torrent of words at the creature and it was only with great difficulty that Inspector James managed to calm the situation.

"Tell him that if he can't sit down he'll be handcuffed! With iron handcuffs!" Inspector James said.

The fairy reluctantly sat down again, after Rowena had translated. Then he said something.

"He says that you have no jurisdiction over him," Rowena said. "He's quoting the Treaty and Covenant, as they all do."

The Inspector sighed.

"Tell him that, as he well knows, the Treaty and Covenant doesn't apply to Fair Folk who are involved in human crimes."

The creatures smiled, baring a set of small, but sharp-looking teeth.

"He says that he has been involved in no human crime. It is not a crime to use one of their vehicles, he says. Filthy things though they are."

"Ask him what he's doing so far from home? What the Cimbriani are doing so far from their domain?"

The creature reacted angrily again to the question. Rachel could see a pattern emerging; the fairy behaved like a petulant child whenever the Inspector revealed any knowledge of it or its people. First it was the language, the fact that they had an interpreter, which had brought an outburst, now it was because the Inspector had demonstrated he knew where the creature came from and who its people were.

The fairy would volunteer very little. When James suggested that he was an outlaw of some sort, the creature responded by saying that he was acting with authority. But he would not say by whose authority. Just when the interview seemed to be stalling, Rachel said:

"Ask him about the girls they were looking for?"

Rowena glanced at the Inspector, who nodded, and Rowena asked the question. The creature grew suddenly still, silent, and then replied that he didn't know what they were talking about.

"We know," Rachel said, "that you and your companions were looking for a group of your women at a club called Havana Nights and that resulted in a fight that left a number of people dead."

Rowena translated and the creature turned its gaze on Rachel, eyes that seemed to threaten or promise deep watery depths from which she would never emerge again.

But the creature would say no more.

Rachel took the Inspector and Rowena back to her station and parked the car.

"I think we could all do with a drink," the Inspector said and though it was the middle of the day, Rachel had to agree. The interview had been something of an unnerving experience; a clash with another world that she had not known existed.

"What did you make of that?" Rachel asked when they were sitting in the pub around the corner from the station. It was one of those old-style London hostelries, not yet modernised or turned into a gastro-pub. The colour scheme – if it could be called that - was brown and so was the general fug of the place, as if centuries of cigarette smoke still hung in the air, the ghost presence of scores of dead drinkers.

"Well, it was to be expected, Rachel," Inspector James answered. "They never give much away. But he was rattled, by what you said."

Inspector James looked at Rachel and she read a mild sort of criticism in his eyes.

"Yes," she said. "I'm sorry I sprung that on you, but I didn't really have time to brief you before the interview. It was a bit of a punt really; a shot in the dark."

The Inspector shrugged, as if to convey that it didn't matter.

"It does put a different perspective on things and would explain a lot."

"So you think that could be it! Some kind of falling out between gangs!"

She presumed that fairies had their own version of organised crime just like humans.

"No, Rachel, you misunderstand me."

Rachel thought that misunderstanding the Inspector wasn't that difficult, as he seemed to speak in riddles.

"I think," he went on, "that this is effectively a rescue party. They are trying to retrieve some of their people. How these people came to be trafficked is a question we can't answer, but I think we can guess who was involved."

"Andy Francis?" Rachel suggested.

"From what you've told me, I would suggest it is likely. That would explain his brother-in-law's abduction."

"So," Rachel said. "These Cimbriani, or whatever they are called, attempted to rescue these women of theirs, but weren't successful. So, they decided to kidnap Tony to use as a bargaining chip!"

The Inspector nodded.

"Yes. That's probably as far as we can go for now."

"We'll have to let our friend go," Rachel said, referring to the prisoner. "Shall I put surveillance on him?"

"If you've got the resources, you could try," the Inspector said. "But one thing these people are good at it is shaking off pursuers, so don't expect much of a result."

"What do we do?" Rachel asked, starting to feel that familiar itch of frustration coming over her.

"We wait, Rachel, to see who makes the next move."

When they had got to the pub, Rowena had disappeared to the Ladies – probably a good move, as she looked so young that otherwise the landlord would have wanted to I.D. her – but that was some time ago so Rachel was now growing concerned.

"Is she alright?" She asked the Inspector, nodding towards the empty place on the bench besides him.

"The interview took a lot out of her," the Inspector said. "Brought a lot of memories back, she just needs time to compose herself."

But Rachel did get up to go and check on Rowena. When she got to the Ladies – all cold, white porcelain steeped in the smell of disinfectant - the woman was staring into the mirror above the wash basin, seemingly miles away. Seeing Rachel, she started and said:

"I'll be there in a minute!" She had a very squeaky voice, Rachel noticed, very high-pitched.

"I just wondered if you were alright," Rachel said.

"I'm fine, now," Rowena replied, but she didn't look fine.

Whatever else Inspector James was good at, he wasn't good at logistical arrangements, and he hadn't put any thought to accommodation for the night. And he was fussy about it.

"I need somewhere secure, Rachel," he said. "Rowena may be at risk."

"From whom?" Rachel asked, somewhat confused.

"From them," the Inspector said. "When they know that she's here, they might want to take her back."

There was no time to ask him what he meant, as Rowena had finally emerged from the toilet. So, they drank up and Rachel, rather reluctantly it was true, decided that the only thing she could do was to take them home to her flat.

She managed to get hold of Ellen – it was after 4pm and though Ellen was still at school, classes had ended for the day – and asked her rather sheepishly:

"Do you mind having a couple of guests for the night, while I sort something out?"

Rachel stumbled over her explanation, because what exactly could she say? Ellen sounded rather dubious about it at first, but then seemed to accept it. After all, Ellen's parents often stayed with them when they came down to London and Rachel had never had anyone stay before, not even a lover, as she liked to keep her sex life separate from her home life.

When he eventually met Ellen, Inspector James was, of course, all charm. He insisted that he could sleep on the couch, so that Rowena could have the spare bed in the study. He had made a call on the way to a supermarket to buy wine and food and he seemed to want to turn the evening into some sort of dinner party.

"I'm really sorry about this, Ellen." Rachel said, when they were preparing dinner in the kitchen. It was the first time they had been alone, since Ellen had come home.

Ellen gave her a rather arch look and asked:

"Do you work with these people? Or did you just randomly invite them home?"

Rachel could see that Ellen found the whole thing more amusing than irritating; if she was in a bad mood about something, she would always show it, but at this moment she seemed intrigued by the whole situation.

"I suppose you could call the Inspector a colleague of sorts. He was the person I went to visit in South Wales. He's up here helping me with a case."

Ellen nodded, but didn't look up. She was in the process of assembling a salad. There was a lasagne and garlic bread in the oven. It was the sort of scratch meal that Ellen excelled at and had insisted on preparing, though Rachel would have probably got another takeaway.

"What about Rowena?" Ellen asked. "She's surely not in the police force."

"I suppose you could call her a consultant," Rachel answered. "That's probably an apt description."

"She looks like she's somewhere on the autistic spectrum to me," Ellen answered and then the oven timer went off and they were taken up with serving the dinner, so they left it at that.

Ellen knew, anyway, that Rachel wasn't in the habit of discussing her work, so Rachel was sure that she wouldn't pry too much.

Dinner was a strange affair, during which Rowena's silence was matched by the Inspector's volubility. He had that easy manner that older people often have of being sociable and relaxed at the dinner table, talking, but not dominating the conversation. He asked Ellen about her job and seemed interested in what she told him; apart from being a class teacher, she was the Special Educational Needs specialist in the school. He even dragged out information from Rachel; about her mother in Oxford and her various jobs in the police. It was only later, after she'd gone to bed, that Rachel realised that he hadn't actually told them much about himself.

It would have been an almost pleasant evening, at least diverting, but for the fact that Rowena was withdrawn and effectively mute for most of the meal. This put something of a damper on the cordial atmosphere. In fact, she didn't last the whole meal and rather abruptly retired to her bed in the spare room, her food half-eaten, mumbling some excuse.

"Is she alright?" Ellen asked the Inspector. "Shall I go after her?"

"Don't worry about Rowena," he answered. "She's not a very sociable creature at the best of times and today has utterly exhausted her."

There was something about the Inspector's voice, its suddenly serious tones, which effectively put an end to the party. Frivolity was forgotten; laughter seemed somehow hollow. Soon after, the Inspector disappeared into the kitchen to wash up – he insisted on it, eschewing the dishwasher, which he seemed to regard as some sort of infernal invention – and Ellen made her excuses and went to bed.

"I've got an early start in the morning," she said.

Haven't we all? Rachel thought.

When the Inspector had finished, they at least had the opportunity to talk about the case, something they couldn't do in Ellen's presence.

"You are probably wondering about Rowena," the Inspector said, pre-empting Rachel's question. He filled up their wine glasses before continuing. It was a school night and Rachel had already had most of a bottle, but she didn't object.

"Rowena," he said, "spent a good part of her early life with the Tylwyth Teg – the Fair Folk - so she speaks their language. It's actually a form of proto-Celtic and I can just about manage to communicate in it, but she's fluent."

Rachel didn't quite understand.

"What do you mean? She was brought up by them?" She asked.

"Not exactly, Rachel," he replied and then sat back, as if considering what to say next.

"It still happens, though it's not supposed to, that a human child is taken by the Fair Folk. It's usually on a whim these days, a pretty child catches the eye, and is then abducted."

"That's terrible!" Rachel said. "How can we let that happen?"

"The answer is that we don't, usually. There are what you might call protocols in place. But the fairies are impulsive, anarchic creatures, so though the whole changeling thing has been discontinued - you know the swopping of fairy babies for human ones – children are still taken."

"But why?" Rachel asked. Her head was spinning, either from the wine or from what she was being told, or a combination of both.

"The fairies have always had a fascination with human children. They'll take them as servants – a bit like the way that aristocratic ladies would have a black boy as a page in the eighteenth century for the novelty value – or as companions. They usually don't mean them harm."

"So, you are saying," Rachel said, "that these creatures live besides us – in parallel to us – and they even take our children!"

"Yes, Rachel. They've always been there, just in the shadows, but generally we co-exist without any major problems. And children that are taken, we eventually get back. As we got Rowena back."

"But she doesn't seem right," Rachel said. "I don't want to be unkind, but she seems damaged almost."

The Inspector nodded and replied:

"It's a traumatic experience being taken from your family, raised in another culture, and then effectively wrenched from that one. And fairy land is different from the human lands. Time progresses differently there. The whole perspective of things is different."

He paused, as if considering his words, and then went on:

"Rowena came back – we got her back – but sometimes I have to call on her for tasks such as this one. I don't like doing it, because it takes a toll from her, but I have little choice."

It was all a bit too much for Rachel. The last few days had been more than overwhelming, they had turned her understanding of the world upside down. So, she went to bed.

Chapter 9

The carpet underfoot was sodden, every step she took the water sucked at her shoes and she could already feel that her socks were wet. She wished she'd worn boots or, much better, wellies, but she hadn't really been prepared for this. The air of the place caught in her throat. It wasn't just the residue of smoke, but a chemical stench of burnt plastic that seemed to hang like a fug over everything. It was made worse by the fact that she had a cotton-wool feeling in her head; not really a hang-over, but approaching one. She had, after all, been rudely awakened by the phone somewhere around 6am.

"Are you awake, Rachel?" The voice had asked. The answer to which should have been: no, not really. "There's been a development."

D.I. Andrews had a wicked way with understatement, Rachel decided, because the development had been an arson attack on one of Andy Francis' restaurants. The 'Becasse D'Or' in Mafeking Street, Islington, was a pseudo-French eatery, frequented by a clientele of the pseudo-rich and pseudo-powerful; in short, the great and good of the borough.

"Did you ever eat here, Rachel?" Andrews asked, as if he was trying to make conversation. When she shook her head, he added:

"I did. My wife and I used to come here regularly. I must admit that I never knew it was owned by Andy Francis."

Rachel could appreciate the sentiment. The 'Becasse' took up two floors of a townhouse in a street of similar buildings. This was a smart part of London. Geographically it wasn't that far from 'Havana Nights', but it was light years away from it in terms of wealth and class. The people who frequented the 'Becasse' either ran the country or had a major stake in it. Nobody cared what happened to the 'Hav', which was basically a brothel, but the 'Becasse' was a different matter.

"Luckily, no-one was hurt," D.I. Andrews interrupted Rachel's reverie, "the place had a sprinkler system and the two floors above are – I should say were – offices and were unoccupied at the time. The fire went up, not sideways, which was fortunate."

Andrews was wearing a pale trench coat over a charcoal grey suit, white shirt and the sort of striped tie that old colonels wore. Rachel didn't think that Andrews had ever been in the Army, so if it was a regimental tie, it probably belonged to some made-up unit. He had swopped his leather shoes – expensive-looking ones - for a pair of green Hunter wellies; he was always prepared like a superannuated boy scout.

Rachel, in jeans, sweater and anorak, with blowsy, wind-blown hair, felt like another species beside him. She hadn't even had time to shower. But she knew Andrews was always well turned out. He was also well-connected; he was heading places, commissioner material, and wouldn't be held back.

"I don't like this, Rachel," Andrews continued. "Murder, abduction and now arson. It's starting to look like a miniature crime wave. And we've got very little to go on."

Andrews didn't have to add that this could seriously affect the division's clear-up rate, which would, in turn, affect Andrews' career prospects. He'd need somebody to blame and she would probably be that person.

"We need to get our arses moving on this," Andrews said, though Rachel knew it was her arse he was actually talking about. "Go and have a chat with Andy Francis and find out what the fuck is going on!"

After the way her last meeting with Andy Francis had gone, Rachel didn't hold out much hope of getting him to repeat the exercise. But, rather surprisingly, before she had even picked up the phone to contact Andy at his business address – the legit one anyway – she had a phone call from his solicitor. Mr. Francis was willing to come in that afternoon to help them with their enquiries.

When she told Andrews, he just said:

"It figures!"

And then she got it. Andy would have had the restaurant insured and to avert any suspicion that it was an own goal – that he had burnt it down for the money – he was prepared to be seen to be co-operative. Until the matter of the insurance pay-out was settled, anyway.

She'd arranged to see Andy Francis at 2pm, but before that she had another job that she had to do. She'd managed to beg and borrow a safe house from the Serious Crime Unit and she was determined to move the Inspector and Rowena into it that morning.

It was obvious that Rowena's presence made Ellen uncomfortable and it was starting to spook Rachel as well, but it wasn't only that. It was more to do with the fact that Rachel didn't think that either Ellen or herself could put up with another night like the last one.

Because Rowena didn't sleep, instead she wandered around the flat, singing or muttering, turning on the taps in the bathroom innumerable times, opening the fridge and the cupboards, switching the kettle on and making endless cups of tea.

At one point Rachel had heard Rowena crying out and had got out of bed to see what was happening. As she came into the living room she could see the girl sitting next to a bleary-eyed Inspector, on the couch he had just woken up from. He was clasping her hands in his and, for a moment, Rachel had the errant thought that there was something physical between them going on. But she abruptly put this out of her mind. The girl was gabbling on in a low voice.

"I can hear them," she was saying. "They are close. They know I am here."

Then she started sobbing.

The Inspector looked up at Rachel.

"It's all right, Rachel," he said. "Go back to bed and try to sleep!"

He looked at Rowena.

"You're having a bad night, aren't you my dear?"

Then he looked back at Rachel.

"It happens," he said. "I'm used to it."

She did go back to bed, but not to sleep. Though Rowena quietened down, there was something too disturbing about the girl and everything that was happening, to allow her much rest. And 6am had come around much too quickly.

The safe house was an apartment in an anonymous block. They were all new-builds, in an equally anonymous North London suburb; all concreted squares and pocket-sized parks. It was the sort of place that ordinary people would struggle to afford and most of the flats were owned by foreign landlords, bought as investments and rented out at exorbitant prices to wealthy students, businesses or as tourist accommodation.

The apartment was furnished in the slick, anodyne manner of a show house; magnolia walls, a shiny metallic kitchen, wooden Scandinavian furniture and high specification electronic equipment. Rowena, who Rachel had had to wake from her bed in the spare room, seemed in a trance as they drove over in the car and disappeared into one of the bedrooms when they arrived.

They decided to let her sleep. Rachel arranged for a uniform – the redoubtable Sam – to drop in and baby-sit her. Then she set out for the station and her meeting with Andy Francis.

"Mind if I attend?" Inspector James asked and Rachel agreed. After all, what exactly could go wrong, she asked herself.

As it was an informal interview, it wasn't taped and Rachel explained the Inspector's presence away by saying he was from another force, following up on a number of other cases with a similar M.O. Francis and his solicitor accepted this without question; after all, it was in their favour if the arson could be pinned on some unconnected party or person.

Predictably, Andy – through his solicitor, who ventriloquised his thoughts – averred that knew nothing about the fire. He also declared – again through his solicitor – that he knew of no-one with a grudge against him. His solicitor, a young, sharp character with a Public School accent and an attitude to match, stated emphatically that Andy was a respectable business man, a pillar of the local community, and a well-known philanthropist.

Rachel wouldn't have been surprised if the solicitor – Daniels by name – had added that Andy was about to be canonised by the Pope, such was the blinding ray of sunlight emanating from his posterior.

Just when the interview was almost over, and they were all standing up, there was a knock on the door and Thomas appeared.

"There's someone on the phone asking for Mr. Daniels. They say it's urgent!"

There was no way that an up-and-coming, self-absorbed, legal eagle like Daniels was going to ignore a phone call. And he was too green and unversed in the ways of the criminal world to recognise the subterfuge. As soon as he had closed the door, Inspector James said:

"Mr. Francis, I want to give you some advice."

Andy Francis looked at the older man, a smile on his face, as if wondering what the fuck the old guy was on about. Because nobody warned Andy Francis off, not even if they were police.

"You're kidding, aren't you?" He said. "Do you know who I am? Do you know who you are dealing with?"

"No, it is you who don't know what you are dealing with. You have no inkling. You have got involved in something which is too big for you this time. Despite all your money and your resources, this will turn out badly for you." The Inspector met Andy's eyes without flinching; it was the gangster who turned away first, somewhat disgruntled.

Just at that moment Daniels came back in, flustered and angry, obviously sensing the fact that he had been tricked.

"This really is not on! Using a pretext to get me out of the room to talk with my client without benefit of legal counsel!"

"Why don't you just shut up!" Andy Francis said. And Daniels did as he was told.

Rachel wasn't one of those people who could hide her displeasure, even with as senior officer. The Inspector had pissed her off; it was that simple. That had been her interview and he had hijacked it. And she wasn't quite sure what he had been trying to accomplish.

"I'm sorry Rachel," the Inspector said, when they had been left alone in the room. "I can see that you are not exactly delighted with my intervention."

One thing that she had to give to Inspector James, she thought, he had no difficulty in reading her.

"It's just not the way I do things, Sir! I don't believe in threatening the people I'm interviewing, not even low-lives like Andy Francis."

The Inspector sighed, suddenly looking tired, as grey in the face as his suit. He must, Rachel thought, have been up half the night with Rowena.

"I wasn't threatening him, Rachel. That was a warning and it was sincere. He really has no idea what he's got himself tangled up in and the Cimbriani can do much worse things to him than we ever could."

Later, when the Inspector said that he needed to get back to the safe house to check on Rowena, she didn't offer to go with him. Quite frankly, the old man was getting on her nerves and she still wanted to have that chat with Andrews about how much he knew and how this all fitted in to their case.

Rachel wasn't sure how to play this anymore. It was Andrews who had put her on to Inspector James and his unit, so Andrews must know more than he let on. She was indeed beginning to wonder if Andrews was deliberately keeping her in the dark on this, avoiding her and feeding her just enough to be getting on with.

She knew that Andrews was a political animal and it could be that, if he knew that there was a good quantity of manure adhering to this case and that there was any possibility of this manure coming into contact with any sort of fan, he was going to be sure that he had his metaphorical umbrella up and if anyone got covered in said manure, it was going to be Rachel, who was more of a natural fall guy than he was.

She sat at her desk thinking. Lunch time came and went, but she didn't feel at all hungry. The inside of her head felt like it was straining to keep all these thoughts in; as full of gunk as a washing machine filter.

It was then that her phone rang.

Chapter 10

Deb had been trying to get hold of D.I. Andrews; he'd given her his card. But D.I. Andrews was not in the office and so Rachel had ended up with the short straw. Or that's the way she saw it. Because Deb wanted the sort of commanding masculine comfort that Andrews could offer; that sort of calm male presence, with an innate authority and just a hint of manly aftershave. And there was no way, obviously, that Rachel could provide this.

Deb wouldn't come into the station; she was a Francis, after all, and wanted to keep her contacts with the police discreet, if not totally secret. Rachel thought that she would probably have rather met Andrews in some sort of louche, private drinking club, with muted lights and over-stuffed banquettes, where she could bathe in his protective glow, but instead she had to make do with Rachel and a Wetherspoons in Holloway. Where she had wanted subtle lighting and a hint of cologne, Deb got the smell of sweat and stale beer. But Deb had been desperate, so she had no choice.

The smell of sweat, Rachel thought, was actually emanating from her own body, overlaid with the after-tang of the burnt restaurant. She looked at Deb sitting opposite her, dressed in a well-cut black trouser suit, an expensive camel coat around her shoulders, all tan and jewelry, and she couldn't help feeling resentful. The wages of sin were supposed to be death – Rachel remembered that from Sunday school – but Deb looked like she was having quite a good time of it.

"I've just come from work, D.S. Stevens," Deb said, "so I can't be long."

"What do you do, Mrs. Francis?" Rachel asked, trying to build up a rapport, just like they told you to do at Hendon.

"I run my own business. A beauty parlour and tanning salon. And please call me Deb!"

It figures, Rachel thought, that would be the sort of job that Deb would do, probably bankrolled by Andy.

"Okay, Deb. Why don't you call me Rachel? Then if anyone overhears us, they won't know I'm on the force."

Deb nodded and then took a pull of her drink; it was a double vodka and tonic. She was nervous and trying not to show it, hoping the booze would help.

"Why did you want to have a chat?" Rachel asked.

"I'm worried about Tony," she answered. "He hasn't come home."

"So, your brother Andy wasn't being totally truthful with us, when he said that Tony had gone on an errand for him?"

Rachel looked at Deb as she said it and saw just a momentary flash of anger in her eyes. She wasn't going to admit that to a copper. And how dare Rachel have the temerity to suggest it, even though it was true. Then, abruptly, Deb regained her composure. She was the respectable, wealthy lady-who-lunched again. It was as if the mask had slipped for a few seconds.

"Andy keeps telling me that it will be alright. That he will sort it, but I'm scared."

She reached for her handbag and opened it.

"I was willing to leave it to Andy, but this was put in the mailbox last night."

She held out a rather grubby sheet of ruled paper.

"Just put it on the table," Rachel said. "We might be able to get prints off it and the less people who handle it the better."

Deb did as she was told and Rachel read the rather crabbed, untidy writing on the sheet.

"Tell Andy," it said, "they want their people back. He knows who I mean. They're not kidding around. They say its blood for blood. They will contact you for a meet. Do what they say or I've had it."

The note ended with a signature.

"I presume that's Tony handwriting and signature?" Rachel asked.

"There's more," Deb said. "There was a lock of hair with it. His hair!"

She held out a clump of dark hair that she'd put in a plastic see-through cash bag; the sort that banks give you.

"Did you show it to Andy?" Rachel asked.

"Not yet, but I will."

"What do you want us to do?" Rachel asked. It was a genuine question, she really wasn't clear what Deb wanted.

"I know what Andy's like," Deb said. "He's not going to trade with these people, whoever they are. He couldn't hold his head up again, if he did. People respect him and are afraid of him. But I'm worried he'll get Tony killed."

Rachel looked at Deb and saw the truth that was at the heart of her. She might dress and act like some sort of footballer's wife, she might even flirt with other men – like Andrews – and even have affairs – perhaps with Andrews, Rachel hazarded a guess, then stopped herself going further – but deep down, underneath, she was the little girl from a terraced house in North London and she loved Tony. He might be a waste of space, her brother's factotum, but she didn't want to risk losing him.

"Okay, Deb," Rachel said. "Here's what we're going to do!"

For once, Rachel actually found D.I. Andrews in his office.

"And so, what did the fragrant Deborah have to say to you?" He asked.

Rachel wondered if Andrews had deliberately ducked out of a meeting with Deb. Perhaps he just didn't want the complications that it might entail.

Andrews, who was lolling in his chair, sat up abruptly when Rachel told him about the meeting.

"Good! At last we're getting somewhere. So, you're saying she definitely agreed to tell us, before Andy knows, where the meet is going to be."

"I think she'd frightened, boss. You know that under that respectable veneer, Andy's vicious and unpredictable. Although Deb won't come out and say it, I think she wouldn't put it past her brother to sacrifice Tony, if it means he can keep up his reputation for being untouchable. You know the score!"

Crime bosses were a bit like sharks, Rachel knew, if one of them started bleeding – showed any sign of weakness – the others would pull it apart. Andy was playing for high stakes and Tony's luck might have just run out.

"We need to be able to move at a moment's notice. We'll need A.R.U. back up, but I want to keep the lid on this. I'm not bringing in the drug squad or the organised crime people. If too many people know about his, we could be compromised."

Andrews was already reaching for his phone.

"You'll tell Inspector James and his .... um, associate. Will you? We'll probably need that sort of expertise."

"I'm on my way now, boss."

Andrews was obviously expecting her to leave, but she hesitated. He looked at her questioningly.

"Boss," she said, "we never had that chat, did we?"

"No, Rachel," he said. "I feel I owe you an apology. I could have prepared you better."

"There's not much you could have said, boss, without appearing barking mad."

Andrews nodded and almost let himself laugh.

"You've realised by now that we have to keep this as discreet as possible. It has to be on a need-to-know basis."

"I understand, boss!" She answered.

"Could you imagine what would happen if the general public got to know that fairies were real and that they were running around in the streets of London waging war on gangsters?"

"It would add another dimension to the immigration debate," Rachel said.

"The fairies are no longer at the bottom of the garden," Andrews continued, "they are in the living room drinking your whisky and watching your TV."

Rachel phoned Sam to tell her that she was on her way and to check that Inspector James was there. The phone was passed from one hand to another and a voice, rather tentatively, said:

"Hello!"

"Inspector James!" Rachel said. "We've had a lead!"

"Oh, I am glad, Rachel," the Inspector said, as if Rachel had just told him that she had passed an exam or got a new Guide badge.

"I'm on my way," she said. "I'll tell you all about it when I get there!"

She arranged to meet him in a pub, just around the corner from the apartment complex. It was an elementary security precaution really, ensuring that the safe house remained, well, safe, as well as anonymous. Traffic was light for once, so she got there early at 4pm. She had forty-five minutes to wait and she thought of phoning Sam again to get the Inspector to meet her earlier, but in the end, she thought that she needed the rest, needed a breather. She could get something to eat, get a drink and try and get her head in order.

It was one of those new pubs that are often built on estates. A modern building, comprising a big open-plan room with a bar in the middle. It had large, picture windows, which let the sunlight flood in. Rachel didn't appreciate this, she thought that pubs should be dark and gloomy, places where you could hide away. It was one of those pubs with an eminently forgettable name – the Jolly Miller or the Valiant Trooper – that wouldn't lodge in your brain, however much you tried to remember it. It served food all day – bland, anodyne, but food anyway – and seemed to be open all hours.

The staff seemed as disinterested as the clientele, but it was a strange hour of the day, Rachel thought, to be in a pub. 4 pm was neither lunch-time nor evening and only committed soaks would be drinking at that hour of the clock. Having said that, the place was full enough; mainly older people, men who looked as if they had been there all day, and a smattering of young, professional types, who'd probably got out of the office early and decided they needed a drink.

Rachel gave the number of the table she had occupied and ordered a burger and a lager. She brought her drink back and settled on the faux- leather banquette, getting her notebook out. She wanted to write down the details of her meeting with Deb, before she forgot them. She'd tried recording notes on her phone or writing them down on her tablet, but she always ended up using the old-fashioned method; pencil and pad. At least you knew that the battery couldn't run out on you, in mid-sentence.

She hadn't noticed the woman sit down at the table next to her. It was only when she started speaking to her that she became aware of her.

"Sorry?" Rachel said.

The woman repeated her question.

"You have the time, please?"

The voice was accented; East European, Rachel thought. You could usually spot the Eastern European women – the Poles, the Hungarians and Bulgarians – they were always friendlier and politer than your average Londoner.

"It's 4.10pm," Rachel said.

"Thank you very much," the woman responded and Rachel glanced up and looked at her properly for the first time.

She wasn't as young as Rachel had thought at first. She had long ash-blonde hair – what you could see of it, because she had a bright red, beret perched on her head and pulled low– and light, greeny-blue eyes. She looked familiar somehow; fine features, arched eyebrows, high cheekbones. She could have been a model if she had been a little taller, but then Rachel thought that perhaps she was a model and that accounted for the familiarity of her face.

"It is quite busy here," the woman carried on talking. "I thought it would be quieter."

Rachel just smiled at her and went back to her notebook. The burger came and she ate it. Every so often, the woman would glance in her direction, but Rachel kept reading and writing; she didn't want to get into a conversation with her; nothing personal, she was just a Londoner like the rest of them, minding her own business.

At half past four Rachel decided she needed to get mentally prepared for her meeting with the Inspector. She headed to the Ladies to have a pee, wash her hands and splash her face. As she came out of the cubicle, the woman from the table next to hers was standing at the sink.

"Oh hello, there," she said.

Rachel nodded and washed her hands, then she scooped some water up into her face and moved over to the electric drier, dripping water everywhere.

"Shit," she thought, "I didn't think that through."

Suddenly, she was aware of a movement behind her; she didn't think that she had heard anything, it was as if some instinct had told her. She turned and saw the woman there, looking into her face and smiling.

God, thought Rachel, is she making a pass at me?

The woman's hand came out towards her, it just seemed to brush the side of her face.

"Look, I'm sorry, but I think you got the wrong impression."

Rachel was going to say more, but her tongue was suddenly too thick in her mouth to get around the words. She started feeling faint and her vision was suddenly telescoped into nothing. Then darkness came.

Chapter 11

Then there was light again, coming gradually back with consciousness. She woke and then slipped back into the void, then woke again, like a swimmer surfacing from the deep, gasping for air. Grasping also for meaning.

Then there was a face, a familiar face. A familiar touch. A voice she had heard before.

"You are a pretty one," the voice said and the face smiled, showing sharp little teeth. "Your skin is so soft and smooth and such a dark colour. Perhaps I will keep you, after all!"

The eyes stared at her, looking down intently into the pools of her own eyes, as if they were drinking them in.

"We are so white, you see, our skin like snow or morning light. That's why some people call us the children of the dawn. But that is only one of many names that we are given."

And then a laugh, so much like music, or like the babbling water of a stream, a mountain brook running fast.

Then darkness again and then light and other voices in a language she could not understand. Then awareness came. She looked around her and saw another figure there, tied and hooded. The figure was sobbing. Realisation came quickly, like a jolt of electricity, a flash of lightning.

"Tony," she whispered. "Tony!"

But somebody else must have heard, because the muttering of voices stopped and a face emerged out of the gloom; it was a face like the one she had seen on the slab. It hissed at her and then retreated.

Then there was another voice, higher, lighter, and more words she couldn't understand and then the woman's face again.

"You have come back to us once more!" She said.

It was the woman from the pub, but transformed. She had lost the beret and her long hair flowed forth, over her shoulders and down her back, the blonde-grey colour of it catching and holding what light there was in the place. It was centre--parted and tucked behind her two ears. It was these two ears that were drawing Rachel's attention; they were rather cute, shell-like, but definitely pointed.

The woman laughed, seeing the questioning look on Rachel's face.

"You have the time, please?" She said. "I was trying to sound like one of you, to look like one of you."

Rachel had started to take in her surroundings; a low, arched ceiling, dark gloomy corners, with a central core of light where other figures came and went and, a short distance from her, the hooded, sobbing figure, bound to a chair. Rachel realised that she was similarly bound; her hands tied behind her, her ankles bound to the chair legs. She had a sharp pain in her neck and she wondered how long she had been slipping in and out of unconsciousness.

"You humans are so gullible," the woman said, "you see what you want to, so it is easy to trick you. To us, you are slow, lumbering creatures and we are as quick and light as butterflies."

She laughed again.

"Are you thirsty?" The woman asked. "You must be, it is always so!"

Then she called out in words that Rachel did not understand and another creature came from the centre of the room – where Rachel thought she could see a table – bringing a jug and a cup. This creature - a male fairy, dressed incongruously like his fellows in a business suit - glared at her and muttered something to the woman and then retraced his steps back to the table.

"Garin said that I should give you drain water. A rather uncharitable way to treat a guest I think."

The fairy woman poured liquid from the jug into the cup – unexpectedly they were both made of plastic – and then looked quizzically at Rachel.

"If I untie your hands, so you can drink, will you give me your oath that you will not try to escape?"

"Fine," Rachel said, "okay, I agree."

"No, you must swear," the woman said. So, Rachel complied, repeating the words that the woman recited.

"You must not break your oath!" She said. "You understand that!"

When the woman untied her, Rachel had to flex her wrists for a few moments to get the feeling back into them. Then she took the cup from the woman's hand, noticing for the first time how long and slim her fingers were. Surprisingly, the liquid was beer. It was warm and flat, but welcome anyway.

"My companions have done nothing but complain since we have been in this city about the ale and the wine. It does not taste as ours does and, besides, they say they prefer mead."

The woman looked at her.

"You know what mead is?" She asked.

"Of course," Rachel said.

"But you Christians no longer drink it? You have quarrelled with the bees?"

She laughed again and Rachel realised that this last comment qualified as a fairy joke. She took a good look at the woman, standing there before her. She was wearing a long dress or robe of some shiny blue material – like satin, but finer – with a girdle around the waist and shoes like pumps on her feet. Hanging from the girdle was a sheathed dagger.

Seeing her looking, the woman said:

"I don't know how you humans stand those tights clothes you wear; they are so hot and uncomfortable. What do you make them of? I can't wait to change, to let my skin breathe."

The drink revived Rachel and did something to dispel the personal fog cloud that seemed to be hovering around her head.

"Did you drug me?" She asked.

The woman smiled.

"No!" She said. "I have no need of potions or draughts. I just cast a glamour on you."

"What do you mean? A spell?" Rachel asked.

"You might call it so, though it is neither as simple nor as complicated as that."

First fairies, Rachel thought, and then magic. It was turning out to be a bad week. And why did they always speak in riddles like this?

"Whatever you used on me, you must realise that you have committed a serious offence. I'm a Detective Sergeant in the Metropolitan Police, not one of Andy Francis' thugs. You need to let me go!"

"Oh, I know all about you, Rachel," the woman said. "I know what you've been up to and that's why I wanted to meet you and have a chat with you."

The woman's speech was a strange mixture of quite formal language interspersed with colloquial phrases, as if it was slightly out of balance and not totally in tune with its audience.

"Who are you?" Rachel asked. She was beginning to feel angry and frustrated. Her neck hurt, her whole body was aching, and just under the surface, starting in the pit of her stomach and spreading out like a cold fire, fear was making its presence felt. God knows what they intend to do to me, Rachel thought. But she knew she had to keep calm, take every moment as it came.

"You know all about me, but what about you. Who am I speaking to?"

The woman looked at her, no longer smiling, drew herself up to her full height and said:

"I am Princess Morgana Gwenhwyfar of the kingdom of Cimbriani, anointed daughter and heir of King Cerwyn of the White Shield and Queen Rhiannon, the Fair-Browed."

Then her face relaxed and a ghost of a smile haunted her lips.

"But you can call me Morgana, for short."

Rachel didn't know what time it was; the creatures had taken her phone – she didn't wear a watch – along with her handbag and her warrant card. She thought that it was probably evening and that she had probably only been out for a few hours, but she couldn't be sure.

Sometime later – minutes or hours, who knew – she was unceremoniously dragged away from the chamber, down a corridor, or tunnel more like, and into what seemed to be a disused, empty storeroom. There was a pallet of sorts here – a thin, strip of foam covered with a blanket – and a bucket, which she had to use straight away – dying for pee again and just glad that she hadn't wet herself, which would have made her situation that much worse. Thankfully, there was light – an electric strip-light – which the fairies had the decency to leave on, so she didn't pee over her jeans.

As they dragged her off, they'd taken Tony away as well, but she soon lost sight of him. She could still hear him sobbing, though.

"What have you done to him?" She asked Morgana.

"Nothing!" The woman said. "We haven't hurt him, but not all Christians are like you and can look into the faces of the Fair Folk without quaking in terror!"

Rachel wished they'd stop calling her a Christian, as she wasn't; they seemed to use the words 'human' and 'Christian' interchangeably.

Morgana came to see her some time later, bringing food, or what passed for food; a take-away burger, fries and a milkshake.

"This is the sort of thing that you Christians eat, isn't? She asked.

Rachel wasn't going to disagree, in case they stopped feeding her.

"Why do you call us Christians?" Rachel asked. "Most of us aren't these days."

Morgana smiled.

"It's what we have always called you, from time immemorial. From when you were all –or almost all – Christians and it was your church that turned the people against us. Said we were servants of your Devil. Said that we wrought evil and mischief."

She paused and helped herself to some of the fries that Rachel was doggedly chewing through, on the basis that, when you were abducted, you ate what you could, when you could.

"So, the name stuck, I'm afraid," she said.

"How do you speak English?" Rachel asked. "How do you speak it so well?"

"We are not unaware of your world, Rachel. And we know that it impinges on our existence. Our continuing existence, I should say. If I am to rule my people one day, I need to be able to understand you, negotiate with you when necessary, so my mother made sure that I could."

Rachel offered Morgana a sip of the milkshake. In the normal course of things, Rachel couldn't be doing with flavoured milk, but Morgana seemed to relish it.

"Finish it, if you like," Rachel said.

"There is more coming and going between our world and yours than you know of or would expect, Rachel," Morgana continued, "and it wasn't difficult to receive an education among your people."

Then she seemed to grow serious.

"You are a good detective, Rachel, as you seem to be finding out things about me. But you are my prisoner and I am the one who should be asking questions. Tell me! The other policeman – Old Grey Brock – how did you get to know him?"

It took a moment for Rachel to realise who she meant, but when she understood, it seemed to her, that the fairy name for Inspector James was particularly apt. He was old, grey and had the stolid, determined air of an old badger. But she couldn't help laughing.

Morgana seemed bemused by this.

"I will never understand you people. You seem to find the most extraordinary things funny!"

I could say exactly the same thing about you, Rachel thought.

Rachel didn't see any need to withhold information from Morgana – she wasn't an S.O.E. agent being interrogated by the Gestapo after all; she had no secrets – so she told the truth.

"Inspector James has come up to London to assist me with this case. He has expertise in these matters, as you obviously know."

"And he brought the woman with him, the runaway. An ungrateful wretch, by all accounts." Morgana said. She was obviously not a great fan of Rowena, Rachel thought.

"I could help you, Morgana," Rachel said. "I know you are looking for some of your people. I suspect that Andy Francis abducted them or inveigled them into working for him. We can settle this without further bloodshed. Let me help!"

Suddenly, Morgana stood up. Though it was hard to read a fairy's face, even Rachel could see the anger that flashed in her eyes.

"So you," she said, "a mere human, think you can render assistance to a full-blood princess of the Cimbriani. That I should be beholden to you!"

"I didn't mean that," Rachel said. "I just meant that I could help to sort this out; get your people back."

"Don't you worry, Rachel!" Morgana replied. "I don't need your help to finish this. I will not only get my women back, but I will also have my revenge. Blood for blood and twice-fold!"

Morgana looked down at Rachel, sitting there on the pallet, the remnants of the meal before her. She had reverted to haughty, princess mode, which, in itself, was something to be seen.

"And if you are lucky, Rachel, if fortune smiles on you, I may take you back to my palace with me, to serve me, to sit at my feet and see to my every whim."

Then Morgana left the room, locking the door behind her.

That was the trouble with fairy princesses, Rachel thought, just when you thought you were getting on with them, even becoming friends, they put you in your place.

Chapter 12

Rachel wondered what was going on in the outside world, if they had even noticed she was missing. In this underworld, she could hear bustle and noise in the corridors outside and, once briefly, Morgana came into her room again. This time she was wearing trousers and boots, with some sort of cuirass covering her upper body, made of small, silver-coloured links. She had also accessorised her outfit with a sword that was belted around her waist. Rachel, oddly, felt little surprise seeing her dressed in this way; the strange had become the commonplace.

"I will talk more with you in the morning," Morgana said. "But you must now rest and keep up your strength."

In a flash, she moved forward and touched Rachel's brow again before she could move away. And the darkness came once more.

When Rachel woke there was some different quality in the air; something she could sense rather than hear or see. For one thing, there was less noise coming down the corridor. The fairies seemed a noisy, querulous lot, given to sudden fits of merriment and then sudden anger, so the silence signified to her that they had gone and left her on her own.

She tried to make a mental calculation of them, to count the number she had seen. She thought that there was probably a dozen of the male fairies, but perhaps more. She doubted that there could be more than twenty, as the low chamber and the corridors around it were cramped and confining. The process was made that much more difficult by the fact that her head still felt foggy and thinking straight was hard.

It must be the glamour thing, she thought. Each time that Morgana had cast it on her, she woke up with what could best be described as akin to a mild hangover; cloth-headed, but also strangely passive, as if she had been robbed of her gumption and will.

At least the glamour had made her sleep, she thought. Otherwise, she never would have got off, worried about rats and whatever other creepy crawlies inhabited the place. She wondered where she actually was. She knew that there was a veritable labyrinth of tunnels under London; disused Tube lines, WW2 barracks, lost rivers, and that didn't even take into account the intricacies of the sewer network. She wondered how Morgana had got her out of the pub toilet, but knowing Londoners as she did, it was possible that no-one had noticed – just another legless drunk, nothing that unusual

She looked around the room that they had confined her in. It did, in fact, look relatively modern, like a storeroom or a lock-up for equipment. Though the walls looked old – Victorian stone-work, she thought – the door was metal, as was its frame and there were metal shelves along the two walls. There was nothing on the shelves and nothing on the floor but rubbish. A discarded newspaper in one of the corners was dated March 29th 1974, which gave her some idea as to when the room was last in use.

Rachel shook her head to try and clear it and then put her ear against the metal door. She could hear a faint murmur and then, surprisingly, laughter. There was, it seemed, still at least one of the fairies left on guard. There was a window-light above the door, of opaque, toughened glass, but it didn't open.

She sat back on the pallet and tried to think. There was no way she could force the door or pick the lock. It was an old-fashioned mortise lock, but it wasn't rusted or worn. The room felt hot and close, though there was some air getting in, an occasional cold blast of it. Suddenly, she realised that the air must be coming from somewhere; there must be an air duct of some sort.

It was, of course, in the ceiling. But though the ceiling of the room was low, there was nothing to actually stand on. Rachel peered up into the grille and inspected it as closely as she could from the floor below. It was obvious, even at that distance, that the shaft behind the opening was narrow; just a couple of feet square. Why, she thought, are there always these air shafts in movies that are so high and wide that people can crawl through them? Even though she was relatively skinny – a runner's body – there was no way she could have crawled through that cramped space.

But something else occurred to her as she stared at the airshaft. She realised that the ceiling was a suspended one, made of panels or plaster board. The room hadn't, after all, been designed to be a cell. She used the shelves that were bolted to the walls as impromptu ladders and tried each of the far corners of the room, to see whether she could loosen the ceiling panels.

The first panel she tried was fastened too securely, but in the second corner, as she pushed, she felt the panel give and succeeded in pushing and shoving it over enough to allow herself to look through. Above her she could see stone vaults that were almost exactly similar to those that roofed the main chamber and the tunnels off it. The storerooms had obviously been built into an existing chamber and the ceilings put in to make them more fit for purpose. From the light that leaked into this loft from her own cell, she could just make out the ceilings of two other rooms and the inner face of a wall of boarding that must close the gap between the outside walls of the cells and the vault above.

It occurred to her that Tony might be a prisoner in one of these other rooms, but she had no way of knowing which and little time to investigate. She had seen a possible gap in the boarding on the far side of the last cell, where the board met the stone walls of the chamber. It was just discernible in the light from her cell and the chamber beyond. Faint hope thought it was, she got her body up through the space she had made and crawled towards this gap, hoping that it wasn't just as shadow or a trick of the light.

She crawled gingerly and slowly, afraid that the ceiling panels might not take her weight and also frightened of meeting some creature up there. It was, after all, the stuff of childish nightmares, stuck as she was in the dark, god knows how far from the world that she knew. But, as it turned out, there was a definite gap. It was a narrow crack, really, where the boarding abutted onto the stone of the wall, but it was definitely there.

She listened at the gap for several minutes. She could still here that low buzz of noise, interspersed irregularly with the sound of muted laughter. She thought it was coming from the main chamber and tried to remember the lay-out of the place. She had still been wool-headed when they led her here, but she seemed to remember that they had come a few yards down a corridor, where a smaller chamber opened out, fronting the rooms they used as cells. This meant, she thought, that the sound she heard was probably coming from the main chamber, not this smaller one, so she could afford to make a certain amount of noise without alerting them.

She had no tools, only her fingers, but as she pried at the wooden boarding it came away in her hands. There must be a leak, she thought, somewhere up in the vault; water had drenched the wood, rotting it, and it crumbled away. The fairies had, rather obligingly, left a lamp burning in the smaller chamber – they might see better in the dark, Rachel thought, but they still needed light – so she could just about see what she was doing.

When she had made enough of an opening, she lowered herself through it, feet first. As gravity took her and she slipped through, she held onto the edge of the cell wall, the top course of the brickwork, and let herself drop as gently as she could. The fall still jarred her back and took her breath away. She was panting, but she knew that it was probably more to do with fear than exertion, though the aftermath of the glamour did seem to have somewhat enfeebled her.

She listened again, but the pattern of noise was unchanged, so she quickly checked the doors of the two other cells. They were both open. One was full of the detritus and general debris which accumulated in such places, the other had a mattress like her own – a sheet of foam really – a bucket and some empty fast food cartons. It must have been where they had kept Tony, she thought.

Looking around the chamber she was in for the first time, by the dim light of the one lamp, Rachel could only see two exits. One was a bricked-up arch, cold and damp to the touch, as if there was water past it. The brick work was old, but sound, so unless she could rustle up a pneumatic drill, she wouldn't be leaving that way. The other was the short corridor back to the main chamber, from where the noise was coming.

She had no choice, she had to take the only route out and brave whoever was there in the main chamber. She inched up the short corridor – more like a tunnel really – keeping close to stone of the wall. Peering around the corner into the chamber, when she got to the end of the corridor, she could see the occupant of the room in a cone of light created by one lantern hanging on a chain from the ceiling in the centre of the room. It was one of the fairies, but he was dead to everything around him, engrossed as he was with the bluish screen in front of him.

It was a strange incongruous sight; the fierce-looking, male fairy, sitting there on an old sofa, sword near at hand, watching a video, the VCR and TV screen hooked up to whatever source powered the place. The pattern of noise now made sense to Rachel; the low-hum was the dialogue of the film or programme the creature was watching. The occasional laughter came from the fairy. Rachel thought that he was watching Mr. Bean.

From her corner Rachel could see another tunnel across the room. There may have been further exits and entrances, but they were lost in the shadows at the opposite side of the chamber and she knew that she would never make it to them without being discovered. She thought that, if she was quiet, she could just slip across the space and head off down the tunnel. She had no idea where she would be heading – and that did frighten her somewhat, the prospect of wandering lost in subterranean London – but anywhere was better than here.

She waited until the creature had erupted in laughter again and then ventured out into the chamber. She kept to the shadows at the edge and, in a moment, was crossing the space, feeling scared but elated as she gained the far side. This, once more, was a vaulted stone-faced passage, yet again more like a tunnel or a mine shaft than a corridor. There was no light here and she inched forward along the wall, until up ahead she seemed to see a dim glow, the absence of darkness more than light.

Then it happened, she tripped against something – an old can, some discarded metal – and there was a clattering noise which sounded terribly loud there in that silent, confined space. Soon after, she heard the noise from the chamber behind her suddenly cease and then came a collection of low sounds, which would have meant nothing to her, if she had not known exactly what they were; the fairy sentinel was up and alert and would be after her in minutes.

She tried not to panic, not to blindly run down that dark tunnel and risk injury to herself; instead she just kept edging forward until she was in another chamber, where the dim light had come from, and this was lit, she saw, by some sort of shaft up above in the vault. Then she heard the sound of footfalls behind her from the tunnel she had just emerged from and she ran down another tunnel in front of her, heedless of where it led.

The feet pursued her. The tunnel she was running in had water on one side – a sewer she thought – and light was again coming from somewhere above. She ran on, slipping a couple of times and, as a result, lurching dangerously towards the brick channel besides her. She turned a corner and knew that she had to stop. If she carried on – on the verge of panic, as she was – the creature would catch up with her, or she would fall and injure herself, or perhaps even get inextricably lost.

There was a bay just to her left; just a narrow vertical gap where the brickwork was recessed. To her right the sewer suddenly disappeared into a shaft, the water cascading down into the darkness. The tunnel ahead of her sloped upwards. She decided to wait. She would surprise the creature, overpower it. But as she had the thought, she realised that in her weakened state she would have little chance against a fairy armed with a sword. She strained to hear those footfalls, but then she heard too much.

She listened again, knowing that sound can be treacherous in such an enclosed space; knowing that her ears might deceive her. But there was no mistaking it. From one side she could hear the fairy advancing, slowly and cautiously, and from the other direction, up the tunnel, she could hear tentative footsteps and the soft murmur of voices. The other fairies were coming back.

Rachel had an infantile urge to shrink back further into the bay she was in, to disappear into herself, just like, when she was a child, she would pull the bedcovers over her head, as if that would hide her from any monster. The fairy was about to turn the corner. She could almost hear his breathing, sense his presence – as if he had some sort of aura of power – but she realised he was hesitating also, listening as she was, to the voices coming up the tunnel. He inched forward and then he was directly opposite her.

Simultaneously, they realised each other's presence. She tried to remember the self-defence training she had received at Hendon all those years ago. She knew that she mustn't give the fairy enough space to wield his sword, so she threw herself at him, grappling with him. He was surprisingly strong and she was embarrassingly weak. He thrust her off him and threw her on her back, a boot on her chest, his blade above her throat. It all happened too quickly for Rachel to register it.

Suddenly, though, she heard the voices again, coming nearer. Then the sound of running feet approaching. The fairy stepped back, sword raised. Rachel pulled herself back into the bay and, to her surprise, saw the figure of Inspector James above her facing the fairy.

The fairy said something to the Inspector – Rachel couldn't understand it – and the Inspector replied in the same language. Then the fairy struck at the Inspector – an easy, rolling movement of his hand, swinging his sword down at the older man. The Inspector raised his stick and parried. There was the ring of metal on metal. It seemed to Rachel that the Inspector's walking stick was no longer a stick; it was, quite preposterously, a sword.

Then something came out of the darkness and struck the fairy on the head. The creature staggered back and the half-brick – because that's what the missile was - fell on the ground besides Rachel. The Inspector pressed his attack on the stunned fairy, who beat a hasty retreat.

Then Rowena was beside Rachel, lifting her up and the Inspector was looking down at her.

"We better not hang around," he said. "In case he comes back with his comrades!"

Chapter 13

Rachel had often passed the little building just off Tottenham Court Road and hardly ever remarked it. It was cylindrical, about twenty feet high, with pipes of some sort protruding from the roof. She had thought – if she ever had had a thought about it – that it was an old kiosk or something to do with the council and therefore, by its very nature, uninteresting.

When they emerged from the shaft and she realised where she was – in front of the supposed kiosk – she was amazed to think that the strange little building was in fact the entrance to this hidden world, which was there right beneath their feet and had, in fact, always been.

When she had told the Inspector that she thought the fairies were all gone, apart from her guard, they had retraced her steps to the main chamber and the cells beyond, just to see if they could find any clues to where they had gone to. Rachel was concerned that the fairy sentinel was lurking somewhere there in the shadows, but it turned out that he had fled.

"I think he was only left there to guard you, Rachel," Inspector James said. "He has probably gone to find Morgana and tell her that you've escaped."

They poked around for a while in the chamber. Apart from the sofa and the electronic equipment, there were some random supplies; food, sleeping bags and the like.

"The Fair Folk make a show of shunning humans and their things, but they make use of them when it suits them," the Inspector said. He paused by the VCR and looked at the tapes that were stacked on the floor nearby.

"But this is a first," he continued, examining one of the covers. "Though I suppose Mr. Bean goes a long way towards reinforcing their view of humans as basically stupid."

The blade of the sword stick was no longer on show, but had been sheathed, and the instrument had again been transformed back into an innocuous walking stick. Not exactly police issue, Rachel thought, but, then again, fairies with swords weren't exactly a standard part of everyday policing either.

"Shouldn't we get a team down here?" Rachel asked. "To go over the place!"

"There's no point, Rachel." The Inspector answered. "They wouldn't find anything useful. And even if they dusted the whole place for fingerprints, what would be the point?"

They found Rachel's handbag, stowed inside a plastic box with various other human items, like a magpie's nest of things the fairies coveted. Nothing had been taken from her bag, though there was cash missing from her wallet.

"When fairies come among humans, they sometime end up wanting what humans have. And they know that money can buy things in this world." The Inspector explained.

Rachel didn't think that it was Morgana who had taken her money – she was too disdainful of humanity in general – it was more likely to be one of her less haughty companions, perhaps the one that liked Mr. Bean.

Rowena seemed to have been somehow animated by her encounter with the fairy. She was no longer sunk within herself, but seemed fired up with a new energy. It was as if she had transformed her fear of the creatures into anger. She had been the one who had launched the half-brick at the fairy and, as a result, had probably saved their lives.

They quickly retraced their steps back to the tunnel where they had met. On the way Rachel asked:

"How did you find me?"

"You have Rowena to thank for that," the Inspector replied.

He told Rachel that when he had turned up at the pub to meet her and she wasn't there, he had waited for a while, but then grown concerned. He had asked some of the staff if they had seen her and they remembered that a woman had collapsed in the Ladies and the person with her had called an ambulance.

"That's when I started to suspect that you had been taken," Inspector James said. "They described you and then they described the other woman, saying she was foreign. So, I contacted Andrews."

Andrews had had the hospitals checked and started a search, going through all the conventional procedures.

"That was all very well, Rachel, and all things that needed to be done. But I tried a slightly different approach."

Rachel had already witnessed Rowena's gift – or curse, to put it another way – without really remarking it. James told her that humans who had been taken by the fairies – especially children – developed some sort of sense of the creatures. In short, they tended to know when the creatures were near. In Rowena this sense was particularly well-developed, so the Inspector had made use of it.

"The fellow that you were holding, Rachel, was followed on his release to Tottenham Court Road, where he supposedly disappeared. I knew, of course, that the Fair Folk tend to gravitate to underground places, especially in a big city like this, so I thought the creature had probably found some entry point to the underworld and tried to rejoin his comrades."

James had taken Rowena to the Tottenham Court Road entrance way, where she managed to track the creature. How exactly, Rachel couldn't even begin to guess, but the vestiges of energy the creature left were like tracks to Rowena.

"I have a map, too," James said. "Something that the Met wouldn't necessarily have access to. It's the London underworld – and I don't mean the criminal underworld, I mean the literal underworld – compiled by colleagues who've also encountered the Fair Folk before in this city."

It surprised Rachel to hear that the fairies had been here before – been running around London – but, of course, it made sense.

"The map is something of a work of art in its own right. Tunnels and shafts have been mapped and marked down over more than two hundred years. There's a whole metropolis of them under the pavements of the city."

James told her that the entrance in Tottenham Court Road led down into an old WW2 barracks and then onwards to some Victorian sewer tunnels and the chambers beyond them, where she had been held, which were much older.

"We would have probably found you, eventually, but luckily you ran into us!"

Emerging onto a busy London street after the quiet of the underground tunnels was rather unnerving, an assault on all the senses. Rachel's phone had just enough power left on it for her to phone Andrews and tell him to call off the search. He told her to meet him back at the station as soon as possible.

"I don't suppose you brought a car?" Rachel asked, but the Inspector shook his head.

"No!" The Inspector said. "I don't mind chasing blood-thirsty fairies through the sewers, but I draw the line at driving in central London!"

They took the Tube up to Holloway Road and walked from there to the station. Rachel was surprised to find that it was still morning. She had been away from the world for less than twenty-four hours, but it seemed like an age. When she mentioned this to James, as they walked along the street, he said:

"It's like that with fairies, dimensions of space and time seemed to stretch and shorten in strange ways."

Rachel hesitated before going on. She didn't quite know how to ask her next question.

"Inspector, that woman Morgana did something to me!"

"She put a glamour on you, didn't she?" Rowena asked.

On the Tube, she had become her old, subdued self again, as if shy of all the noise and activity around her, all the people. But she perked up again now, at the mention of Morgana's name.

"How can you tell?" Rachel asked. She felt uncomfortable, as if Rowena knew something very intimate about her.

"Once it's been done to you," James said, interrupting, "it's not hard to recognise the signs in another."

"But what is it?" Rachel asked. "It can't be ... magic? Can it?"

"You can call it what you will," the Inspector said "It's hard to explain in human terms. But if you had to try, you might say it was something akin to hypnosis, more of an imposition of will on another person than some sort of spell."

They walked on, turned the corner and were on the station steps.

"You knew her name when I mentioned it, Inspector! Didn't you?" Rachel asked.

He nodded.

"Princess Morgana is something of a celebrity in the world of Faerie, it's true."

"She seemed to know of you, as well!" Rachel said.

But then there was no time to talk as they were through the station doors and Andrews was there on the threshold waiting for them.

He was his usual business-like self. Deb had been in touch, he told her, the meeting had been set up between the Francis gang and the other party – he didn't seem to be able to get himself to say fairies – in a disused warehouse at an old canal dock, north of Regent's Park. They had a few hours to stake the place out and make their preparations.

"Good to see you're back in one piece, Rachel!" He said rather gruffly to her as they left the station, his only demonstration of anything close to emotion.

Rachel told him about Morgana and Tony Francis in the car on the way. She left out the bit about the glamour.

"So, it was the Inspector who found you," Andrews said, laughing. "And I've had a large proportion of the Met chasing around after you."

Rachel, herself, couldn't see the funny side of it

"And Rachel," he continued, "you know better than to put any of this down in writing, don't you?"

Chapter 14

Rachel could see why Morgana had chosen the canal dock. This part of the canal wasn't one of the more trendy areas, with their bespoke houseboats, cafes and markets. This was a forgotten arm of the water-way, a relic of the city's industrial past that had been lost to memory, situated in a wasteland of derelict industrial sites and scrubby woodland that had colonised vacant plots.

The dock itself was set back from a disused lock and the murky, greenish water of the canal. The waters didn't look navigable to Rachel; as if they needed cleaning out and reclaiming. The dock itself was a simple, grassed-over rectangle of land protruding out into a basin, surrounded by what had once been a warehouse, buildings that looked like some kind of offices and a block of old garages or boathouses – they were so dilapidated it was hard to guess what they had been.

All these buildings were in an advanced state of decay. They lined the dockside and behind them was a grassed-over area of tarmac, fronted by a road, which led through the old industrial plots back to a main road. A fence had been erected at the roadside and a sign told any curious passers-by that the land had been acquired by a developer and would sometime in the future be transformed into desirable canal-side apartments. An artist's impression informed the eye of the beholder of the utopia to come; all glass and balconies, neat little houses on tight plots with greenery edged in the angles; smiling children and tall, healthy looking mums and dads, making perfect families for these toy-box dwellings.

That might be the future, Rachel thought, but the present was all wrack and ruin. And the ruined buildings gave plenty of cover, the broken ground a variety of approaches. Morgana obviously had the eye of a military tactician, but then, Rachel thought, she did seem to be some sort of warrior princess.

The location of the rendezvous had, however, caused Andrews something of a headache, for these very reasons. It seemed logical that the Francis crew would approach down the road in vehicles, but it was equally unclear how the fairies would approach the place. Then there was the question of numbers. The information that Deb had given them – from the second scribbled note that had been pushed through her mail-box – had just a location, the name of the place - Mafeking Dock. There were no conditions made; no talk of how many men Andy Francis could bring with him. Rachel thought that either Morgana didn't care or she knew that Andy was unlikely to play it straight anyway.

In the end they set up surveillance on the top floor of the warehouse, with another team in the undergrowth at the end of the road. There were two squads of armed police, waiting in vans and ready to go, just up the road in the ruins of factory, a few minutes away. Andrews fussed and fretted about the resources they were expending – this was uncharacteristic of him, he was usually as cool as the proverbial cucumber – which Rachel knew was a sign that he was worried.

Andrews had baulked at bringing the Inspector along, but in the end, he had been persuaded. The man was, after all, some kind of policeman; basically, one of them. But he wouldn't have Rowena there, saying it was too dangerous for civilians. She would wait in the station to assist officers with any fairy prisoners they brought in.

The information from Deb had been sketchy. They knew little more than that she had received that other note, placed in her mail-box, again written by Tony. Andrews was at something of a disadvantage as he hadn't actually seen the note, but had just had its contents read out to him over the phone by Deb. He didn't want to incur Andy's suspicions by meeting Deb in person, at least that's the reason he gave, though Rachel thought he might be avoiding the woman for his own, personal reasons.

In the note, Tony had said that 'they' wanted to set up an exchange of 'prisoners'. As if, Rachel thought, they were Cold War spies and not North London gangsters. He'd signed off by saying that it was his last chance. Almost begging, according to Deb.

"The fragrant Deborah is very worried about her hubbie," Andrews said as they sat up on the top floor of the warehouse. "She's afraid that it's curtains for him if Andy doesn't play a straight bat and she knows Andy too well to think that he will."

Rachel stole a quick glance at Andrews. There was no doubt that he was a good-looking man, she thought, personable and charming. But there was a hardness underlying all that charm. He'd led Deb on, flirting with her, providing the shoulder to cry on that she needed and now he was keeping her at a distance, keeping her needy. It was like a fisherman paying out the line before reeling it in. He obviously had little but contempt for the woman, but she was shaping up to be a good source for him. Still, Rachel knew that Andrews was a good boss and a good leader, even if he was basically a bastard.

They had a good view of the tarmac area in front of the warehouses through the window they were sitting at and, just across the floor, another window looked down at the dock itself. They had found a couple of old chairs – the tubular metallic kind, with hard wood panels for back and arse – so it was just like they were watching a movie in a cinema, seats aligned, the screen before them.

"What's your plan, Inspector?" Inspector James asked his counterpart, Andrews. He was a little way back from them, seated where he had a good view out of the second window.

"My intention," Andrews answered, "is to observe what happens and then to intervene when needed. If all goes to plan and an exchange is made, we'll move in afterwards, intercepting both parties separately. If things go pear-shaped – which they probably will – we'll intervene then, but I don't want my officers getting caught in the cross-fire. We'll stand back until we can act decisively."

Inspector James nodded his agreement.

"That's what I expected," he said, "but be warned that the fairies will appear suddenly and depart quickly. It's the way they fight. And they are out for revenge. They lost one of their own."

"Andy Francis lost a good few men, dead or maimed, perhaps that will be enough for them," Andrews said.

"No, it won't," the Inspector answered, "they don't reckon one human life, or even several, as equivalent to their own lives and there's also the question of the women that were taken."

"Well," Andrews said, a slight tone of irritation penetrating through his professional composure, "I presume these creatures are just as vulnerable to bullets as we are. They're not super-heroes, for god's sake. Are they?"

"You're right, of course, Inspector Andrews," James replied. "They can be killed. But, in fact, they are more robust than us and heal more quickly. They move faster and regard us as clumsy and lumbering. Don't underestimate them!"

The radio crackled out an end to the conversation. Two Range Rovers were approaching down the access road, sandwiched between them was a white Transit van.

Andrews gave them a running commentary:

"One of the Range Rovers has stopped and pulled off the road. There are four guys getting out of it and deploying. They are carrying long bags – as if they are fishermen carrying rods – but our surveillance people think that there are guns in the bags."

A statement of the bleeding obvious, Rachel thought, but kept it to herself. The other Range Rover and the Transit van drove up and stopped at the gate in the wire fence – where a man got out and used bolt cutters on the padlock – then drove in and parked on the tarmac. Four men got out of the Range Rover, but the driver of the van stayed put.

Carefully and slowly, Rachel moved to stand by Inspector James at the other window.

"Any sign of the fairies, Inspector?" She asked.

"I haven't seen them, Rachel," James answered, "but they are already here."

Rachel looked at him askance.

"I can sense them," he said.

A cold feeling went through Rachel as he said it, somewhat akin to that sense of dread that grows in your guts when you are terribly afraid. She was remembering Morgana, being in the woman's power, being helpless. She made a conscious effort to suppress the feeling.

Then they heard a plaintive voice, calling out below them.

"Andy?" It asked. "Where's Andy?"

After that, after those words, it was hard to know exactly what happened; hard to string together random events into some sequence that made sense.

There was gunfire below; what sounded like hand-guns – single shots – and then the staccato of some kind of machine gun. Andrews was at the window, binoculars in one hand, radio in the other, when suddenly the panes around him erupted in a shower of glass – the window was broken already but there were still jagged shards in the frame – and metal fragments.

"Fuck!" He said and went down.

Rachel moved back towards him, but Inspector James, with a surprising burst of speed, grabbed her arm and stopped her.

"Keep down, Rachel!"

She threw herself on the floor and crawled toward Andrews followed by the Inspector.

"I'm alright," Andrews was saying. "I just can't see probably."

They had a first aid kit with them – standard practice on that sort of operation – and Rachel broke it open and found a dressing. It wasn't Andrews' eyes that were the problem; his sight was obscured because blood was flowing into them from a head-wound, which in itself looked nasty. One of the fragments of metal had also pierced his upper arm.

Rachel fumbled with the dressing, but eventually managed to strap up Andrews' head wound. Then she heard a noise behind her. It was the Inspector, moving towards the stairs.

"Inspector James!" Rachel called, but he was already gone.

"Go after him!" Andrews said.

Rachel followed the Inspector down the stairs. She could still hear the sound of gunfire outside the building she was in; the walls around her seemed to provide scant protection against the chaos outside. She wondered if she was being foolish, running towards the bullets, instead of running away from them. She had been in some dangerous situations before - drunks swinging punches, three occasions when knives had been brandished at her, one incident when a depressed farmer had threatened her with a shotgun – but she'd never actually been caught up in a fire-fight. Part of her wondered how she would react; hiding in a cupboard seemed preferable to heroism.

The Inspector disappeared around the corner at the bottom of the stairs and headed down a corridor; she caught up with him at the external door. Only then did he seem to see her, to realise that she had been following him.

"Keep down, Rachel!" He said, crouching at the door jamb.

She looked questioningly at him, but he just said:

"Morgana!"

And then she saw the fairy woman out in front of the dock. Tony Francis was hooded and shackled, both hands and feet, and Morgana was leading him, like a dog on a lead, as he shuffled along. Behind her were two fairies with crossbows – Rachel had seen such things in films, but never in real life – who seemed to be covering her retreat.

Just as Rachel caught sight of her, Morgana spotted Inspector James. She had a fierce, savage look on her face and she barked some command to her two body-guards, who turned their crossbows on them. Rachel crouched down against the door; the cover was sparse, but better than nothing. But Inspector James stood up and walked out into the open space, holding up one hand and shouting something.

The fairies paused, looking to their princess for instruction.

"Stay out of this, Inspector James!" Morgana said. "You may call truce, but I've had enough of human perfidy today!"

The two male fairies were armed with swords, as well as their crossbows. Morgana only had a sword, but an extremely mean attitude to go with it. Rachel feared that the Inspector would be cut down on the spot. She, herself, was only carrying an extendable baton and pepper spray; standard procedure, as they always left the really rough stuff to the armed response team. She should have stayed where she was, radioed in for back-up, but instead she found herself standing and walking out towards the Inspector. It was an act of will, almost unconscious, and courage or cowardice had little to do with it.

Morgana suddenly saw her, as if for the first time:

"You should have kept out of my way, Rachel!" She said. "You have displeased me enough already!"

"You know me, Morgana, or at least you know of me!" Inspector James said.

Morgana looked at the Inspector as if debating whether to kill him immediately or wait until later. Rachel had the baton in her right hand; she was trying to plan a course of action. There were three of them and she didn't fancy her chances against the crossbows. She thought it was best to go straight for Morgana, to close with her. They wouldn't dare fire at their own princess, she hoped.

"Be quick with what you have to say, old Brock!" Morgana said. "I'm in a hurry and you are starting to tire me!"

Rachel could hear the sound of tyres screeching at the front of the warehouse; something was happening.

The Inspector ignored Morgana's jibe and kept on speaking calmly.

"You didn't really expect Andy Francis to play fair, did you? You were prepared for treachery."

Morgana smiled and said:

"Of course, I was prepared! I know what Christians are like! I've grown to expect it!"

"So you know that it is unlikely that you will get your women back this way again!"

Morgana didn't answer, but he had her attention now.

"I can get your women back, Morgana! Without any more of this senseless violence!"

"And why should I believe you, Inspector? Why should I trust you?" Morgana asked.

"There are two reasons, Princess. Firstly, you know my reputation amongst your people. Secondly, you are acting outside the Treaty and the Covenant and the consequences could affect us all."

Morgana smiled and laughed scornfully.

"I'll give you three days, Inspector," she said. "Then I rain down fire."

Abruptly, she turned her back on them and started walking away.

"What about Tony?" The Inspector asked.

"The dog stays with me!" Morgan answered, not deigning to turn around. "And I'll have his head at the stroke of the midnight hour on Friday, if you do not return our womenfolk."

Morgana and her companions stepped into the woodland and brush behind the dock and seemed immediately to vanish.

Chapter 15

The Range Rover lay forlorn and abandoned, all its doors thrown open. There were three bodies around it; all brought down it seemed by crossbow bolts or arrows. The other occupant, Rachel thought, must have got away, but how far he had got was anybody's guess.

The Transit driver had made an effort to escape, but the tyres had been shot out as he tried to turn the vehicle around, again by arrows. Quite a feat of marksmanship, Rachel thought, though she knew little about archery.

"Bodkin arrows!" The Inspector said, as if he had read her thoughts. "Developed to pierce armour, so quite effective on tyres and, it seems, modern forms of protection."

Rachel could see what he meant. Most of Andy Francis' men had been wearing some sort of body armour, but it hadn't saved them.

"The fairies developed the longbow, Rachel – that's where the Welsh got the weapon from – and it's a formidable weapon in their hands, though they are also pretty effective with crossbows as you have seen. Morgana's people are warriors and the Francis mob are thugs; vicious thugs, it's true, but not trained soldiers."

Rachel could see the truth of what he said in front of her, where the ARU people were trying to piece things together, to make sense of the scene.

It was Andrews who had called them. While she was chasing after the Inspector, he had got up off the floor, picked up his radio and binoculars and – under fire – had guided them in. It was the sort of thing Andrews would do, she thought wryly, why he would be Commissioner one day and she never would. Because she had acted on impulse and he had done his job in a cool, detached way.

Andrews had had a free ride out of there in an ambulance. He was going to lie in a hospital bed for a couple of days and be feted as a hero, while she would probably end up being disciplined for leaving her post, such was the way that life – her life anyway – went.

"I don't know what they are going to make of all this," James said. "They'll probably put it down to the work of Chinese Triads or Hungarian Roma, something exotic at least."

He was perceptive, Rachel thought, that was basically what it had been written up as last time. They were drinking mugs of coffee – vile instant stuff which she would have normally loathed, but today was welcome – sitting on the back step of the Transit van. There'd been nowhere else to sit and it wasn't exactly a crime scene. The crime scene was a hundred yards away where the driver's headless body lay. He'd run for it, but hadn't got far.

Rachel knew that the fairies would have been incensed when they opened the van and found out that the women weren't in it. It was pretty obvious they wouldn't be, but there was always a slim chance. But the driver hadn't been afforded even a slim chance; they'd taken their anger out on him.

Sitting there, talking to the ARU people, she had managed to piece together what had happened. While they had been setting up in the warehouse, the fairies had come – silently and ghost-like – and taken up position around them. The Francis gang hadn't been firing at Andrews, but at the fairy archers who were above him on the roof top, he'd just got in the way.

In fact, the whole strategy of the Francis gang had gone wrong from the outset. The occupants of the second Range Rover, the one that had detached itself from the convoy, had been supposed to set up a flanking manoeuvre, coming up behind the fairies with a hunting rifle and a Kalashnikov. But they'd been outmanoeuvred themselves, running into a close quarters ambush where their weapons were of limited use, and were last seen running for their lives through the labyrinth of abandoned industrial sites.

The four guys in the Range Rover had lost their back-up right from the start. They had emerged from their vehicles assuming that they would have a parley and, when the fairies were off guard, they expected their back-up to take them out. Morgana had sent Tony out, as a distraction, shuffling along in his hood and chains, but then the fairies had almost immediately fired on the Francis boys with devastating effect.

It was, as the Inspector said, the result of untrained thugs going up against soldiers, but one thing bothered Rachel.

"What if the women had been in the van?" Rachel asked. "The gang could have shot it up!"

"Morgana knew that they weren't there, she wasn't guessing!"

"What do you mean?" Rachel continued. "Is she telepathic?"

"More like a heightened sensitivity," the Inspector answered.

Rachel could see that some of the ARU lads – who were also having a coffee break – were giving them funny looks, so she said:

"Time to get out of here, I think!"

Back at the station, all was chaos; phones were ringing, officers from different squads were arriving and leaving and orders were being shouted out. The problem was, as Rachel realised, that nobody actually knew what the hell was going on. On the face of it, a gang war had erupted in North London and every squad and unit wanted in on it. The Drug Squad were annoyed that they hadn't been kept in the loop – the Francis clan were, after all, major players in the business – and the intelligence agencies were starting to make interested noises on the basis that this amount of violence and death must be related to terrorism in some way.

Rachel slipped into her office as surreptitiously as she could. Thomas was at his desk, a solid, unmoving rock fixed in that sea of activity. Rachel wondered, again, if he ever left his seat.

"There's a DCI from MIT looking for you," Thomas said, a rather gleeful tone in his voice. It was acronym city at the station, so many different units and ranks. "She's pissed off that Andrews ran an operation without informing her, as it was obviously tied up with the Havana Nights killings."

Rachel knew the score. Andrews was in hospital, a veritable hero, so somebody was going to have to take the blame, but she didn't have time for MIT at the moment.

"If anybody asks," she said. "Tell them that I'm visiting Andrews in the hospital, following up on a lead."

"But the DCI was very insistent!" Thomas said.

Rachel didn't answer. She was already sorting out the files she needed from the filing cabinet and copying other documents onto a hard drive from her PC.

It was outside visiting hours, but she managed to persuade one of the nurses to let her into the ward. A warrant card could get you into nearly anywhere. Andrews was out of bed, sitting in a chair in a small cubicle off the main ward. He was in a surgical gown, with a dressing gown thrown over it. His head was almost totally swathed in bandages and he had one black eye and a bruised face. She couldn't see the wound on his arm, it was obscured by his clothes, but he seemed able to move.

"It's much worse than it looks," he said, which momentarily shocked her, but then she realised that he was joking.

"I'm just waiting for my prescription," he continued, "and then they're discharging me. I've just got to come back in a week's time to the outpatients' clinic."

"It could have been worse, boss," Rachel said.

"Well, they weren't actually aiming at me, but I might have been safer if they had been, given the standard of their marksmanship!"

Rachel told Andrews about the offer the Inspector had made to Morgana. Andrews winced, as if the revelation had made his injuries worse.

"I don't know if he was wise, promising that, but he may have stalled things for a while."

"That's not all, boss," she said. "We've got MIT on our backs as well!"

Their conversation was interrupted by an auxiliary, who had brought Andrews's prescription. Then Rachel waited outside the ward for him as he dressed – or was helped to dress – and was discharged. As they walked along down the corridor, she noticed that his jacket – a green waxed Barbour imitation – was still flecked by the dark stains of his own blood.

"I'll have to get it dry-cleaned," he said. "I wonder if the blood will come out!"

Rachel thought that Andrews probably had a wardrobe full of such clothes - suits, coats, tweeds - all carefully picked out and styled to give him that cachet of class and background that was something of an essential to get anywhere in Britain these days. For a working-class Kelvinside boy, he was making a good fist of it; you could have easily taken him for a public school kid, a sort of posh Scot.

There was another of those ubiquitous chain, coffee shops in the foyer and they sat down to finish their conversation.

"Can I give you a lift home, boss?" Rachel asked.

"No, thanks," he answered, "I'm going to go back to the station, to write my report and square things with MIT."

She didn't bother disagreeing with him, telling him to go home. Andrews was the classic workaholic. There was probably nothing at home for him, but daytime TV and the fleeting ghost of his marriage and subsequent divorce.

"You work with James," Andrews continued, "and see whether you can locate the women. Then we'll take it from there. If MIT do catch up with you, just say that we were investigating a possible abduction and that we had no reason to link it with the Havana Nights."

Rachel sipped her coffee and tried to fight off the feeling that was gradually creeping over her; she was beginning to feel overwhelmed.

"But how can we keep all of this from MIT, boss? They are bound to find out!"

Andrews winced again, as if his physical pain was inextricably tied up with her words.

"When it's over – if it ever is – we'll give them an acceptable version of events, something that can be explained, but at the moment we can't level with them. You know that!"

She did. Because how would you go about informing a raft of DCIs and Deputy Commissioners that they didn't only have the crimes of a city of nearly 9 million people to contend with, but also a whole undiscovered species of demi-humans, who were none too sympathetic to humans and their foibles. You would either end up causing a collective, national nervous breakdown, or, conversely, be sectioned and committed to an asylum as some kind of lunatic.

The Inspector was waiting for her at the safe house. Rachel sent Sam back to the station; she was getting bored with her baby-sitting duties. Sam was one of those hyper-active young women who had difficulty staying still and she didn't relish the role of bodyguard. Besides, Rachel thought that Morgana would have no reason to move against them or Rowena now. In fact, the opposite was true, she would leave them to try and find the girls. What worried Rachel was what Morgana would do if they weren't successful; the fairy's concept of revenge seemed wide-ranging and all-embracing.

Before she dismissed Sam, Rachel asked her to keep her eyes peeled and her ears open for any clues as to the fairy women's whereabouts on the streets around the Hav. She didn't have much of hope of finding anything out this way – Andy Francis had a zero-tolerance policy with informers – but anything was worth a try.

Rachel spent the rest of the day going over files with the Inspector, both paper copies and electronic ones, finding out everything they could about Andy Francis and his associates. She had hoped that the Inspector might have his own unique way of finding the women; that Rowena could do the same thing she had done when they were searching for Rachel. But the Inspector told her they needed a trail of some sort, an energy trace.

"And the trail is cold, Rachel!" He said.

The problem with Andy Francis was the sheer amount of information relating to him that was out there, both on the files that had been kept, but also on the internet and in the press. Modern life was like that, Rachel thought, everyone created a forest of information, so finding some particular tree in that forest was well-nigh impossible.

They tried to narrow it down.

"We can presume," the Inspector said, "that the women are being kept at a secure location, but I doubt that it is in the immediate area, or Morgana would have found it by now."

Rachel didn't ask how, she knew that Morgana had abilities that she hadn't even started to fathom yet.

"This is not unheard of, Rachel, you know," the Inspector continued, "fairy women being trafficked for sex. There's a certain type of man, with a jaded appetite, who would pay an astronomical amount for something so exotic. But it is a speciality, offering such a service. The clients aren't going to be satisfied with a glorified brothel like Havana Nights. It will be an exclusive venue, discreet, probably guarded."

"That would fit in with what Sam's source said," Rachel interrupted, remembering what Magda had said to the young woman. "She said they were being taken out of town for rich clients."

"So, it will be somewhere like a hotel or a country house. The latter I would think, to keep things discreet. Andy Francis seems to have a lot of rich friends, so perhaps we should focus on them. See if any of their properties fit the bill."

The more they looked though, the more they found out that, although Andy was on the face of it well connected, many of the great and good had the sense to keep him at a distance. He was invited to fund-raising dinners, hunt balls and the like, but there were few invitations to more intimate occasions.

"He's obviously the sort of bloke you might find useful for business, but wouldn't invite home to your wife or family," Rachel said. She almost felt sorry for poor Andy; he'd never really make the grade with these people. Almost sorry, but not quite.

"He does seem to have a circle of acquaintances, though," the Inspector said, showing her a picture on her laptop. It was Andy Francis in full shooting regalia – a little too full, a little too tweedy – holding a Purdey shotgun, standing in a group of similarly-attired people. They were posing in front of what looked like a Grecian temple, built on a rise above them, besides a lake.

"That doesn't look very English to me," Rachel said.

"It's probably some sort of folly," the Inspector answered. For a moment Rachel thought that he was referring to Andy's tweed plus-fours.

There were approximately nine individuals, not always together in the same group, but linked to each other through photographs taken at various social events. One was a peer of the realm; another an M.P. tipped for political success; two of them worked in finance in the City; one was from a publishing family; the others seemed to have not set profession, but plenty of money to fund their leisure.

"There's a pattern here," James said. "They all live close to, or have country houses near, Cotterham, a village in the Cotswolds. Andy Francis has a cottage there, too."

Cotterham seemed the picture postcard sort of English village that you got in those more expensive and exclusive parts of the countryside. The kind of places where the locals had been priced out of the housing market and where, even if they could afford to live in the locality, there weren't any jobs for them to do. Rachel could imagine Andy, dressed for the weekend in what he thought the country set wore, acting like the local squire. Because, as it turned out, his country house was more of a mansion than a cottage.

"He wouldn't be stupid enough to run an operation like that out of his own property," Rachel said. "But it might be worth checking!"

But they had little time and almost no resources. They couldn't hare off from London on the off-chance that the women were at Andy's country residence. They worked all afternoon, by sifting through documents and searching the Internet, but got no further, As the light was starting to go and Rowena – who hadn't exactly been active, spending most of the day languidly sprawled on the sofa – switched on the lamps and they drank the last of a series of interminable pots of coffee, the Inspector said:

"You should go home, Rachel, and get some sleep. We won't get any further tonight, so let's make a fresh start in the morning."

He saw her to the door, a gesture that was part of his old-fashioned politeness.

"By the way," he said. "I didn't thank you for backing me up today, back at the canal dock."

"You seemed to be quite capable of taking care of yourself! And, by the way, what did you say to Morgana?"

"I called a truce and a parley. The fairies still subscribe to the medieval protocols of war, so I figured that Morgana would respect the convention."

"It looked like you were taking a bit of a chance to me," Rachel said. "And what was that about the Treaty and Covenant. I've heard you speak about that before."

The Inspector looked at Rachel as if considering her question. Then he seemed to make a decision.

"You'll probably need to know this sort of thing, Rachel. The Whitehaven Treaty of 1635 was signed by the representatives of the Fairy Kingdoms and King Charles the First to formalise and enshrine in law the existing covenant between faerie and the human world. It allowed for parallel and separate kingdoms of fairies and humans and set down laws and regulations concerning human-fairy relations."

"And this Treaty has remained secret all these years?" Rachel asked.

Inspector James nodded.

"Since 1635. It survived the Civil War and the Commonwealth. It was renewed by William and Mary after the Glorious Revolution and reiterated by Queen Victoria."

"But who knows about all this?"

"Very few people, Rachel, for obvious reasons." The Inspector said. "If it became common knowledge, it might lead to any number of unfortunate incidents, even civil war."

"I'm just amazed that it has been kept secret for all these centuries! It's unbelievable!"

"Well, in fact, Rachel, people have been reporting sightings and interactions with fairies for centuries. It's only relatively recently that people have stopped seeing them and meeting them; now it's more likely to be aliens they think that they have come across, which is good cover for the fairies."

When Rachel checked her phone before she got in the car, she realised that she had missed two calls from Ellen. So, she made a quick call before setting off, telling the woman she was on her way home.

On the drive back, she felt guilty. She hadn't come home last night and she knew Ellen would have been worried. She should have phoned her that morning to explain. They were only flatmates – she didn't actually owe her an explanation - but she'd never stayed out all night before without telling Ellen. It was just the way they were with each other.

Looking for a parking space in the street outside her flat, she realised how tired she was. Well, she thought, she had been abducted and then in a fire-fight, so it hadn't been an ordinary couple of days at the office. Ellen was sitting watching the TV when she walked in.

"You look exhausted Rachel," she said, after a few moments silence.

"I am exhausted," Rachel said and suddenly she felt that terrible sort of bone weariness you sometimes feel, when you've let go of all that tension, that will power that is keeping you upright. She felt like crying and Rachel wasn't usually a weeper.

"Sit down and I'll get you a glass of wine. There's some sort of pasta bake in the oven. I threw it together, but it should be just about edible." Ellen said.

"Did you make enough for me?" Rachel asked in a rather pitiful voice.

"Yes, of course. I wasn't sure when you'd be in, so I made something that could be easily heated up."

Rachel knew that Ellen would never ask the question, so she came straight out with it.

"I would have rung you last night to tell you I wouldn't be home, but I was tied up!" Literally, Rachel thought.

"That's okay, Rachel." Ellen said, her voice even. Ellen never seemed to get upset, she was always calm. The only way you could tell that she was displeased with you, was by picking up on those little nuances of hers; the occasional sigh, the sideways look, the tut of disappointment. It could be extremely aggravating at times.

"I just thought you might have met someone, especially after what you said the other day."

Rachel considered what Ellen had just said. She did sort of meet someone, but it was not exactly a love match. Morgana wouldn't be someone you would want to have any sort of relationship with, though she was quite fascinating.

"It was an all-nighter at the station," Rachel lied, "and I just didn't have time to phone."

Ellen waited on Rachel for the rest of the evening, so Rachel supposed that everything was alright between them.

The phone woke her up the next morning. She looked at her clock. It was 7.45am. Sam was at the other end.

"Sorry to ring so early," Sam said. "But there's something I need to tell you!"

Rachel phoned Inspector James at the safe house as soon as she got off the phone. He took ages to answer, but eventually he did.

"Inspector," Rachel said. "I think I know where they are!"

Chapter 16

Before them the parkland formed a perfect green carpet stretching to the lake and the temple beyond. An avenue of trees led the eye down to the water and the folly above it, all perfectly proportioned.

"Very Arcadian," Inspector James said. Rachel wasn't sure what he meant, but she wasn't going to ask him.

They were parked off the narrow B-road which passed the estate and looking through the bars of a wrought iron gate that opened onto a track that led to the back of the property. To Rachel, it was a mansion, but the Inspector had informed her that, technically, it was a hunting lodge and not really meant for year-long occupation.

It was the mock classical temple, the folly, that had identified the place. That, and Magda.

Because Sam had been listening to Rachel when she asked her to keep her eyes peeled and ears open to any rumours about Andy Francis and the fairy women. And Sam had done more than keep on the alert. Instead, she had sought Magda out – she wasn't that difficult to find, they had a strict shift rota at the Hav - and bought her a few drinks.

Magda had eventually – after three double vodkas - told her about the parties at the place in the country that Andy Francis used to host for friends and business associates. Mostly posh people, Magda said. She told Sam how he had bussed the girls in for what were basically weekend orgies. She didn't know exactly where they had gone – how could she have – but she always remembered the lake and the temple above it in the grounds. It wasn't the sort of thing that you would easily forget.

Coincidence, lucky break or fate, whatever it was, Rachel was glad to accept it. An Internet search had identified the place; it wasn't difficult, there weren't that many classical temples above lakes in England and fewer associated with known friends of Andy Francis. The house was owned by the younger son of a viscount – a louche character who had a number of cautions for drug possession and a conviction for assaulting someone in a brawl – and, as it turned out, one of Andy's companions in the picture that framed the lake and the temple in the background.

The temple – folly she should call it – wasn't actually that impressive, when you looked at it closely. It was built to appear ruined; a few columns, some standing and some broken, a fragment of portico and roof. Romantic and ruined were the words that best described it. A waste of money, Rachel called it. But by all accounts the family had had cash to spare, all amassed from sugar and slaves. A questionable past never did most of the aristocratic families of the land much harm.

"We'd better not linger," the Inspector said. "In case anyone gets suspicion."

Rachel knew what he meant; the country wasn't always that friendly, there was always someone who'd pop up from behind a hedge to tell you off for reversing in their driveway or taking a wrong turn down their track. People with property wanted to protect it.

They got back in the car and drove down the road and past the main gates; Rachel slowed as much as she could without drawing undue attention to them and their vehicle. The Inspector turned to Rowena, who was in the back seat.

"Is there anything? "He asked.

"There's something," she said. "It's not clear, but there is something."

They checked into a small, anonymous hotel just outside Cotterham. The hunting lodge, Dunstan Park, was approximately 10 miles away from the village to the west. Tony Francis's house was a few miles away from the village in the opposite direction. It was a small village, so they wanted to attract as little attention as possible. They had constructed a cover story - academics on the way back from a conference, taking a scenic detour, thus allowing for a certain eccentricity in appearance and manner – but the young woman receptionist was consummately professional and didn't pry.

Unpacking her toothbrush and the few other items that she had brought, Rachel realised that they were faced by something of a dilemma. The house was owned by the son of a rich, influential family; old money and old power. It shouldn't matter, but it did. These people could marshal a phalanx of lawyers at the clicking of their fingers. But that wasn't the most difficult factor.

The Inspector was quite convinced that there were fairies on the property. Whatever Rowena was picking up – and Rachel wasn't quite sure how it all worked, whether it was like a sort of radar or something more subtle –was unclear, even scrambled, but was tangible.

"Rowena normally describes it as hearing the fairies' voices in her head," the Inspector explained to her. "I think it's more that she has sensitivity to their thoughts and thought patterns, something that she got attuned to in her years of captivity. So, if the signal – if we could call it that – is weak, it could mean the fairies are asleep or drugged. The point is that she is sensing something."

Rachel was willing to take his word for it, just hoping that he was right; she didn't want to be part of a massive cock-up. Because, apart from this tenuous evidence, they had nothing to go on. They knew, or thought they knew, that Dunstan Park had been used by Andy Francis before as a glorified brothel, but that, in itself, didn't signify much. It didn't do anything more than suggest the possibility that it was being used for a similar purpose now.

Rachel could hardly get a warrant to search the place on these grounds. And what would be the basis of the warrant? To raid the place in case there were trafficked fairy women on the premises? She would not relish explaining that to a local magistrate. The operation would have to be a covert one.

She and James had decided that they needed to mount some sort of surveillance on the place to see what they were up against. They were fast running out of time – they had about 30 hours left – but they needed some sort of intelligence. When they drove past the gates, Rachel had noted the electronic gates and the CCTV cameras, but they had not seen any security guards or the like.

The ten mile stretch of country between Cotterham and Dunstan Park was mainly farmland, but as the land sloped up, this gave way to woodland which abutted onto the parkland. Inspector James had gone out and bought a small-scale map of the area. Rachel had offered to get a map up on her phone, but the Inspector had said her preferred an actual, paper map, something he could open up and spread out, as he put it. From the map they could see that it was possible to approach the Park through the woods. It would difficult to do at night, but there were a number of usable footpaths and bridleways.

They left Rowena in the hotel – she had become anxious again, spooked by the presence of fairies – and drove back towards the house. Rachel had all the basic kit they needed in the boot of their car; waterproofs, binoculars, two-away radios, rope and tools. They had to stop at a garage on the outskirts of Cotterham to fill up with petrol - extortionately expensive, Rachel wished she'd got fuel at the supermarket they'd passed as they turned off the motorway – and they had one rather unnerving moment when a car passed them on the B-road up to the house and the driver bore more than a passing resemblance to Andy Francis. He didn't seem to recognise them though.

They parked at a forestry car park and hiked up the hill that overlooked Dunstan Park. To any onlookers they were just people out for an afternoon's walk, but they skipped off the footpath and set up at a vantage point in low scrub, where they could look down into the park and at the house beyond.

They spent most of the afternoon watching. There was nothing out of the ordinary. A food delivery van arrived at about 4pm and half an hour later a car emerged through the electronic gates. There were some groundsmen at work and somebody washing a car in the courtyard behind the house, otherwise it was quiet. They saw a couple of burly-looking men crossing the courtyard, dressed in suits. They could have either been servants or security, but Rachel guessed they were the latter. Partly because they didn't seem to be in a hurry to get on with any work, pausing instead for a cigarette and a chat.

They packed up as the light was going and walked back down to the car.

"I don't think we are any the wiser," Rachel said.

"Well, at least we know the lie of the land," Inspector James answered.

Rachel knew that, however little they knew about what they were going into, they had to raid Dunstan Park that night.

"We'd better get back and make our plan of attack," Rachel said, turning on the engine.

The Inspector nodded and said: "Yes. My people should have arrived by now."

They had almost got into an argument over it, on the journey up. Rachel had always done things the proper way, 'by the book' as all the movies put it. So, she had not been pleased by the Inspector's stated intention to bring in his own unit. They were a rather shady, buccaneering lot and the whole thing didn't sit well with her sense of what good police work should be.

"We have do things properly!" She said to James." Follow the correct procedures!"

"It is debatable what the proper course of action is in these circumstances, Rachel," he replied. "Theoretically, we should be referring the whole matter to the local police, as you know, but I doubt that would get us anywhere. Even if we doctored the story somewhat, it would still be either too flimsy or too far-fetched to warrant their interest."

She knew he was right; whatever she told the local force would be filed away and not acted on. It was all basically rumour, with no foundation in fact.

"You should also bear in mind, Rachel," he continued, "that I have UK-wide jurisdiction in these matters and a remit to take appropriate action."

"But even so, Inspector," Rachel replied. "You have to go through channels, don't you? You can't just mount a commando raid on the place."

"You're right Rachel. I should inform the authorities. The ones in the know, at least. But if we delay, Tony Francis is dead and god-knows-what chaos Morgana will wreak on the rest of the Francis clan and anyone who gets in her way!"

In the end, she had reluctantly agreed to go along with him, but she nearly baulked when they made the rendezvous with what he called "his people". They had arranged to meet them in a car park, on the edge of Cotterham, next to a rather run-down and almost defunct diner – all plastic and glass, now tawdry and smeared – a strange relic of the sixties stranded on the edge of the otherwise pristine village.

There was an anonymous white van and a Land Rover, which had seen better days. When they arrived, the occupants were all standing around, drinking take –away coffee and eating take-away food from the adjacent diner. It was a fine sunny evening, still light, so no-one would think this abnormal; just a couple of passing vehicles pausing for a coffee. Not abnormal, that is, unless they looked too closely.

The driver of the van was the one that bothered her most. He was similar in build and size to the man she had seen with James with on that first day in Abermannan. In other words, built like a brick-shithouse, as her old duty sergeant used to say in her cadet days. He was young, hulking, and hairy. He had long hair and a beard that filled his face and – she suspected – an equally hirsute body. What had James called the man he'd been in conversation with in the old hospital at Abermannan, Rachel asked herself? One of the mountain people, she thought he had said. She had made the presumption that he was talking about travellers. Now she wondered.

The young man greeted James with a rather formal, but awkward, handshake; James solemnly returned it.

"Hello, Carreg," the Inspector said. "I'm pleased that you came!"

Of the other two of the Inspector's people, one was a small, thin creature that Rachel thought was a boy at first. She was dressed in jeans and a fleece jacket with a woolly hat pulled over her head and nearly covering her eye-brows. Rachel had seen enough of the creatures to know that the girl was a fairy; that pale skin, the green eyes, and the ethereal quality that hung around her like a bad smell. The other person Rachel knew already.

"Hullo, Rachel," Rajma said and gave her a hug, which Rachel returned; she was strangely pleased to see the young woman.

The Inspector went in to get them a coffee and Rachel walked over to a picnic table with Rajma, the other two trailing behind.

"I didn't think this was your area of expertise," Rachel said to the woman, smiling.

"It isn't really," she replied, "but we're rather short-staffed at the moment."

Rachel sat down on the bench and Rajma sat beside her. The picnic bench was in the sun and Rachel let the warmth play on her face. She was still tired – was in a state of permanent fatigue it seemed – but the heat was soothing and somehow nourishing. The other two sat down opposite them.

"This is Carreg, by the way," Rajma said, introducing the man-mountain. He glowered and grunted at Rachel and then returned to his food. Rachel noticed that he basically had two meals in front of him.

"Carreg's a bit shy," Rajma said, smiling at the young man, who glowered even more. That's putting it mildly, Rachel thought; he's got no social skills whatsoever

"Ceridwen," Rajma went on, turning to the fairy, "this is Rachel, a sort of colleague of ours."

 Ceridwen didn't even turn to look at Rachel, but just vaguely waved an arm at her.

"I know who she is," she said and that seemed to settle it.

The Inspector came back with two coffees and two Danish pastries.

"Well, they're all eating," he said apologetically, "and lying out on a wet hillside doesn't half improve your appetite."

He let them eat, waited for Rajma to clear away the others' rubbish and then spread out the map.

"You all know why we are here," he said.

As soon as he spoke there was some sort of transformation in his audience; Ceridwen, who had been looking bored and unhappy, suddenly straightened up and became interested; even Carreg, who Rachel couldn't help thinking of as slow-witted, seemed to snap to attention; Rajma, of course, was focused and attentive, always the good student.

"I'll set out the plan," the Inspector said, "then I will take comments and suggestions. Then we finalise it."

They had agreed to rendezvous that night at one of the car parks in the tract of forestry next to the house. This would be their jumping off point. It was conveniently hidden from both the house and the road, the trees and undergrowth forming effective screens. When Rachel pulled up in the car with the Inspector and Rowena, the Land Rover and the Transit were already there, waiting for them.

Rowena slipped out of the back door, before Rachel had fully stopped, and ran towards the others, flinging her arms around Ceridwen.

"I thought she didn't like fairies," Rachel said to Inspector James.

"As they say these days, Rachel, it's complicated," the Inspector replied. "It was Ceridwen that got Rowena away from the fairies and, as a result, she is regarded as a renegade by her people."

James ignored the display of affection between the two women and moved towards the back of the Land Rover. From a metal chest there he took two radio sets, giving one to Rajma. He also handed out torches, plastic restraints and canisters of some sort of pepper spray.

"Just in case," he said. "I shouldn't have to remind you, however, that though this operation is sanctioned under the Treaty and the Covenant, we have to adhere to the law. So, you use only reasonable force to defend yourselves."

Turning towards the young fairy woman, he said: "And no swordplay, Ceridwen. Keep it in its scabbard, unless we're in mortal danger."

It was only then that Rachel noticed that the young fairy woman was wearing a sword on her belt, balanced by a dagger on the other side. Carreg, she saw, had his own weapon; a knobbly, heavy, wooden object that looked like it had been torn forcefully from a tree. That must be what an actual cudgel looks like, Rachel thought, so much more than just a bog-standard club.

"You've got your baton, Rachel?" The Inspector asked. She nodded and then looked at Rajma, who was empty-handed.

"I'm not into weaponry!" The woman said, seeing her questioning glance. "I'm more the book type."

"So," the Inspector said," we synchronise our watches and then we go!"

They waited for what seemed like an eternity by the wall that enclosed the Park. The wall itself wasn't that high and easily scalable with the collapsible ladder they had brought, but it was covered by sensors and infra-red cameras. Carreg and Rajma had gone off in the Transit to the front gate. Carreg, who might look like a Neanderthal, but was apparently "very good with electricity", according to Inspector James, would cut the power for exactly five minutes. This would not be long enough to cause much of a panic, but would probably be put down to a brief, random power cut.

As soon as they saw the house lights go out, they climbed over the wall. Ceridwen went over effortlessly, hitting the ground softly on the other side and then disappearing into the darkness, scouting ahead. Rachel followed, pausing at the top to help Rowena, who seemed too frail for this type of work. The Inspector, she noted, managed well enough himself, though he breathed a bit heavily when he gained the ground on the other side.

They moved off into the parkland. Rachel and the Inspector had seen dogs that afternoon; two hulking beasts, mastiffs of some sort, Rachel thought, though she wasn't a dog woman. It hadn't seemed to perturb the Inspector at all, but it was the thing that Rachel feared the most. There was something primevally terrifying about being attacked by such creatures in the darkness. Now, crouching there as they tried to get their bearings, Rachel heard a snuffling noise and the scrabble of claws on earth, all those little sounds that together told her that the dogs were near and coming for her.

Except they weren't. As they moved forward across the grass they came upon Ceridwen, standing in a half-crouch over the two mastiffs rubbing their ears. She said something to the creatures and, abruptly, they both lay down on the ground and went to sleep.

"Fairies and dogs!" Inspector James whispered to Rachel, as if she should know exactly what he meant.

They kept off the paths, in case there were sensors, and made their way along a hedge towards the courtyard at the back of the house. The lights in the rooms at this side of the building were on and the courtyard was flood-lit, but the front of the house was in darkness, apart from some external lights. The lake, which lay on the other side of the courtyard to them, was wreathed in a mist, which made it look otherworldly, and the folly, rising above it, seemed to have emerged from some past time and impinged on the present.

"They're here," Rowena said. "Somewhere here!" But she couldn't tell exactly where.

As they were moving along the outbuildings that flanked the courtyard, they ran into their first security guard, or, rather, he ran into Ceridwen, who was a few yards in front of them. The man had stepped out of a door, cigarette in one hand, lighter in the other and come face to face with the fairy. You had to give it to him, Rachel thought after the event, he had acted quickly and instinctively, dropping the cigarette and lighter and punching the fairy in the head, aiming for the face, but missing and giving her a glancing blow to the temple.

"Ceri!" Rowena cried and the man, in the process of reaching for his radio, froze for a few seconds in surprise, his hands going instead towards a holster on his belt.

Rachel ran forwards, extending her baton as she did so, and hit him squarely on the right arm, following up with quick sharp strokes to each of his legs. Then, suddenly, Ceridwen was on her feet again and touching the man's face. He collapsed, as if pole-axed. Rachel remembered what it felt like, having a glamour put on you.

"Thank you, Rachel," Ceridwen whispered. It was the first time that the woman had done more than acknowledge Rachel and it was almost touching.

"You seemed to be handling things okay by yourself," Rachel answered.

"No! He was reaching for a weapon and I was off-guard!"

Rachel made a mental note that she should accept gratitude where it was offered and not argue about it.

They tied the guard with restraints and taped his mouth; he shouldn't wake up from the glamour for a while, but it was by no means an exact science. The weapon that he had been reaching for wasn't a gun, but a taser of some sort. Rachel took it along with her, thinking it might come in handy. Then they moved off towards the courtyard, but Rowena paused and kept looking at the lake.

"They are not in the house!" She said. "They're over there!"

"How can that be?" Rachel asked. Rowena was an enigma to her and this vaunted power of hers was even more of a mystery.

"Rowena doesn't get these things wrong, Rachel!" Inspector James said.

They heard the next security guard coming – he was entering the courtyard form the direction of the house, passing through the gateway - so he didn't stand a chance against Ceridwen, who put a glamour on him.

Watching her carry out the task, Rachel wondered at the ease with which she did it.

"Can all fairies do that?" She whispered to the Inspector.

"No, not all," he answered. "In fact, very few!"

There wasn't time for more questions. They found the door to the suite of rooms that were the kitchen, laundry and utility areas. Ceridwen tried the handle and it opened. The guards had probably left it unlocked while they did their rounds, Rachel thought, sloppy, but understandable.

"We'd better split up," Inspector James said. "To cover more ground!"

But then they heard the sound of someone singing to themselves - a young woman's voice - and they heard footsteps coming down the corridor from the main house.

The young woman – Rachel thought she was a maid – was as surprised as they were. She was about to scream, but Ceridwen moved behind her and put a hand over her mouth.

"If you make a sound," she hissed at her, "I will hurt you very badly. If you do what you are told, no harm will come to you!"

They had to get the girl to sit down, her eyes were like saucers, and she was red in the face and seemed on the point of fainting.

"Where are the women?" Ceridwen asked. The girl's eyes flickered, she seemed on the point of lying, but Ceridwen drew her dagger and said:

"Lie to me and I'll stick you!"

"There's no need for the knife!" Inspector James suddenly said, stepping forward. "This young lady will help us, I'm sure!"

And she did. The young woman – Rachel thought she was Polish or possibly Russian, by her accent – told them that the girls were being held in the tunnels.

"What tunnels?" Rachel asked.

"The tunnels that run from the cellar to the lake!" The woman answered, as if it was quite a common phenomenon.

"They are old," she said, "from some club they had here!"

"Like the Hellfire Club, I suppose," the Inspector said. "Or clubs really! Places where gentlemen met for what were basically orgies in the eighteenth century. There are quite a few of these old houses with vaults or caverns built for that specific purpose."

The girl nodded at his words, as if they somehow exonerated her of any involvement in the affair.

"Take us there!" Ceridwen hissed again in that low, sibilant whisper of hers that was all threat.

The maid told them that there were two entrances to the caverns; one in the cellar and one that gave out below the folly onto the lakeshore. The lake shore entrance was chained up and not used. Before the girl took them to the cellar stairs – with Ceridwen close behind her, her very presence threatening harm if she was crossed – the Inspector radioed to Rajma and told her to bring the Transit in through the back gate – where they had stood that morning – and by the track to back of the courtyard.

"We do not know what state the women are in. They may not be able to move very quickly," the Inspector whispered to Rachel in explanation.

A wide staircase led down to the cellar and a sub-corridor with various doors. The maid chose one – unlocking it with her bunch of keys – switched the light on and took them between racks of wine bottles to a further door. This was a double door of ancient looking oak planks.

"Behind there," she said and seemed reluctant to go further.

"They're there," Rowena said. "They're definitely there!"

"So is someone else!" Ceridwen said and then the girl made a run for it. Ceridwen tried to grab her hair, but failed. Trying to avoid the fairy's grasp, she collided with Rachel, who managed to get a hold on her and wrestled the girl to the floor. But before Rachel could stop her, the young woman let out a sort of wail, calling for help.

By the time Rachel had got her gaffer tape and restraints out, Ceridwen had moved over and put a glamour on the girl. Though this took longer than usual, as the maid struggled against it.

"She had a strong will!" Ceridwen remarked afterwards. "But not stronger than mine!"

138

She smiled and showed a set of small, but sharp-looking teeth, as she said this. But then they simultaneously heard two things; the oak doors were creaking open and, somewhere, though it sounded far away, an alarm was going off.

A man erupted from the doorway, holding a taser and aiming at Rachel, the first person in his line of sight. He hadn't seen the Inspector, who lifted his stick up – he was never without it, it had even come on their afternoon hike – and brought it down hard on the man's lifted arms spoiling his aim. Before he had recovered Ceridwen moved to his side and was struggling with him, trying to put a glamour on him, when a second man appeared in the doorway levelling a shotgun at them.

"Stay where you are?" He shouted, but he couldn't fire because his mate was in the way. Rachel lifted the taser she had taken earlier, pointed it at him and said:

"Police! Lower your weapon!"

It was a bit of a bluff. She didn't actually want to taser him as she knew that the electric charge might cause his fingers to twitch and pull the trigger of the gun involuntarily. But the man hesitated, probably calculating whether she was actually a police officer and, if so, whether it was worth his while to shoot her.

"What have you done to him?" The man asked, seeing his friend suddenly crumple to the floor and now pointing the gun towards Ceridwen. He was slowly walking forward.

"Police! Drop your weapon!" Rachel said once more and he turned toward her again, just as the Inspector shoved the open door hard against him. The man, taken unawares, stumbled and fell dropping the shotgun, which discharged. There was a deafening noise in the enclosed space, like the gates of hell opening, and the acrid smell of burnt gunpowder and smoke. When the smoke cleared, Rachel could see that Ceridwen had once more done her job and put the other guard out.

"Is everyone alright?" She asked.

"I think we're all fine, Rachel!" The Inspector said. "But the Chateau Lafitte '88 has suffered a mortal blow."

As he said it, she realised that the shotgun pellets had hit a rack of bottles behind them and smashed them to smithereens, flooding the floor with wine.

"It's criminal waste of good wine," the Inspector said.

They heard footsteps and activity from the kitchen.

"We'd better get moving," Rachel said.

They pushed the two guards out of the way and closed the oak doors from the inside, locking them and leaving the key in the lock, in case someone had a spare. They were in a rock-cut chamber, a sort of guard room, equipped with a table, chairs and a couple of sleeping cots. There was shelf against the wall with a hot plate, a kettle and a small fridge.

"All mod cons!" The Inspector said. "They've definitely made themselves comfortable!"

The tunnel walls had been cabled for lighting and power, so they could see, in front of them, beyond the guard room, a tunnel with steps climbing upwards.

"We should get a move on," the Inspector said." I don't know how long it will take them to get through that door!"

There was a telephone on the table – some sort of military surplus field telephone – and it was buzzing, as if it was angry with them. Rachel knew that it wouldn't take the rest of the security guards long to realise that it wasn't going to be answered.

Rowena led the way now, with Ceridwen close behind her. Despite the Inspector's earlier instructions, the fairy had now drawn her sword. All caution had gone. Rowena was rushing ahead and Ceridwen, though she had vainly urged Rowena to be careful, hurried after her. The Inspector and Rachel brought up the rear.

The tunnel suddenly ended and they emerged into another chamber; a strange, rather remarkable place. It was a high, domed space, probably a cavern in the rock below the folly, which had been enlarged at some stage, the walls being smoothed and plastered. Frescoes had been painted on the plaster, though in place the damp had damaged the pictures or the plaster itself, exposing the bare rock beneath. The frescos could be, at best, described as erotic, or, at worst, described as pornographic. They were obviously old – probably original eighteenth century, Rachel thought – because all the women seemed to be rubicund and voluptuous nymphs or shepherdesses, either being chased by or coupling with a variety of satyrs or demi-gods.

Set in the walls of the chamber were small cell-like rooms, cubicles lined with cushions or mattresses, some quite high up the walls and reached by steps, and the main room itself was floored and carpeted and scattered with divans and sofas of various kinds.

"It looks like somebody's fantasy of an oriental harem," the Inspector said, but Rowena had crossed the floor quickly and set off towards another tunnel cut into the far wall. They followed her. This tunnel descended for a few yards and then branched into three. One tunnel went ahead and continued descending, the other two led off to the left and right. Rowena paused, as if not knowing which one to take, confused for the first time since she had entered the place. By tacit agreement, Ceridwen took the left branch, followed by Rowena, and the Inspector took the right followed by Rachel. Then the lights went out; the guards were trying to make it as difficult as possible for them.

The Inspector switched his torch on. In front of then was a short corridor that led to a door. It was a modern metal security door that jarred with its surroundings, an anachronistic intruder from the present. Rachel could hear a dull, thudding sound, that seemed to be far away, but insistent.

"They're starting to break the door down," she said, realising what the sound was.

"Then we should hurry," the Inspector replied.

The door wasn't locked, but bolted and barred, so Rachel had little trouble with it, but as she pushed it open, something came out of the darkness beyond and sprang at her. Whatever it was, it hissed like a cat, and knocked her backwards off her feet. Hands with sharp nails flailed at her. Instinctively she turned from the mouth and teeth of the thing, which were biting at her face, elbowing its pale face as she did so.

The Inspector barked something in a language she didn't understand and then moved forward trying to pull the creature – which had coalesced into a young, fairy woman – off Rachel. Two other fairies were hissing at them from the doorway of the cell, ready to pounce, but suddenly another voice intruded, low and commanding. It was Ceridwen. Abruptly, the creature on top of Rachel stopped struggling and sprang back and one of the other fairy women moved forward and put her arms around the girl.

Rachel looked around and saw that Ceridwen was standing in the mouth of the tunnel, with Rowena and four other fairy women behind her, all dim forms huddled there in blankets. The three fairy women in front of her, lit by the Inspector's torch, looked gaunt and ghostly. They were naked except for blankets they kept trying to cover themselves with. There was an unpleasant smell emanating from the cell, rather like a mixture of cat's piss and shit, Rachel thought, and the fairies' faces were grey and dirty, their fine hair matted and limp.

"Christ!" The Inspector said, the one word summing up succinctly what Rachel felt.

Ceridwen said something else and the fairy women came forward out of the cell. One of them had to be supported by the two others. The fairies with Rowena were also in a bad state. They had difficulty walking and looked dazed or drugged, apart from seeming half starved.

They were now crowded in the mouth of the three tunnels and the booming sound behind them sounded even more insistent, as if the guards had put on a spurt of speed as they realised that they were on the point of breaking through.

"It's no good going back that way," the Inspector said, "we can't chance it. We don't know how many of them there are or what weapons they've got. We'll try this tunnel."

He indicated the middle one, the one that descended.

"It should take us out to the lake!"

"But the maid said it was locked and barred!" Rachel said. "We could be trapped!"

"We've got no choice," the Inspector answered.

The Inspector set off down the tunnel, Rowena following. The fairy women, understanding finally what was happening, drifted along after them. But Ceridwen stayed put.

"Aren't you coming?" Rachel asked.

"No!" She replied. "I'll stay here for a while!"

"Then I will too!" Rachel answered. She was, after all, the police officer and if anyone was going to be the rearguard, she felt it should be her.

Ceridwen smiled. Rachel couldn't figure out if the offer had pleased her or she just found it amusing.

"No," she said. "You go!"

She said it casually, almost languidly, as if they were talking about getting an ice cream, rather than fighting off their pursuers.

"I'll be along shortly. Besides, I've got a score to settle!"

So, Rachel left her.

The tunnel felt cramped with all of them in it, but it soon opened out into a larger cavern. Beyond the cavern was another tunnel that descended sharply towards the lake. At the end of it, there wasn't exactly light, just a softening of the subterranean darkness.

Rachel and the Inspector left the fairies in the cavern and crept forward. It was, as they had thought, the exit to the lake, but the low, arched gateway was secured by a barred grille, hinged, but chained in place. There were no guards outside. They were hardly necessary.

The Inspector clicked his radio on.

"Rajma," he asked, "where are you?"

She gave him her location.

"We are at the exit from the caverns on the lake shore! Meet us there! I've got a job for Carreg!"

Rachel thought Carreg was going to rend the chain apart with his bare hands. He didn't. In fact, he used a crow bar and worked on the hinges of the grille, that were set in the rock. They were rusted and eventually popped out. It was still, however, a prestigious feat of strength.

"There's a lot of activity around the house," Rajma said. "We should be quick!"

Rajma had driven the Transit as close to the exit as she could, but there was still a couple of hundred yards to cover. Luckily, it seemed as if nobody at the house had entertained the possibility that anybody could get out that way, so they hadn't posted any sort of guard. Rajma told them however, that there were a couple of guards patrolling the perimeter on quads. Rachel was starting to wonder how many guards there actually were. They had knocked out four. How many more could there be?

Rajma started leading the fairy women towards the Transit, while Carreg stood on guard. But Rowena wouldn't follow.

"What about Ceri?" She asked. "I won't leave her!"

"Neither will we," the Inspector said. "I'll go back and get her!"

"No!" Rachel insisted. "I will!"

The Inspector flashed her a brief smile and led Rowena off after the fairy women.

Rachel passed the broken grille and started up the tunnel. She had only gone a few yards when she sensed, rather than heard, someone coming towards her.

"Ceridwen," she whispered, hoping she had pronounced the name properly.

Suddenly the fairy girl was beside her.

"I'm glad you said something," she whispered. "I was wondering whether to stick you or not! I thought you might be one of guards."

They retraced their way back to the exit.

"Are they close behind?" Rachel asked.

"They were!" Ceridwen replied.

"Did you have trouble?" Rachel asked

"No, but I gave them something to think about!"

Rachel didn't understand. Ceridwen laughed.

"I got them to seriously consider whether they were paid enough to take me on in the dark!"

It was a squeeze getting everyone into the Transit and Ceridwen had to sit in the back with the fairy women to reassure them. They had had enough of closed vans and enclosed spaces and they took some persuasion. Rowena wouldn't leave Ceridwen's side and Rajma climbed in the back as well.

Carreg drove the van back up the track, with the Inspector and Rachel in the front seat. Though they were half-expecting to be stopped, they had no difficulty getting to the exit gate and the road. The guards were still stumbling about in the caverns, chasing fairy ghosts.

They drove back to the forestry car park, where they had left the Land Rover and Rachel's car and that was where they ran into trouble. As they were retrieving their vehicles, a squad car drove into the car park, blocking the exit road.

"Police! Stay where you are!" A voice called out.

They all froze in the headlights of the police car, but Inspector James was unfazed.

"Police! Stay where you are!" He shouted, confusing the two constables in the car. Then he moved forward flashing his warrant card. "Code word Ice Fire! Radio it in to your Chief Constable now!"

There was the inevitable delay as the message got passed up through the chain of command. The two police officers – a young woman and an older male sergeant – had got out of their car and were carrying out a desultory conversation with the Inspector. Rachel had remained standing by her car, talking to Rajma. Ceridwen, along with the fairies and Rowena, had stayed out of sight in the van.

"You're a long way from home, Sir," the sergeant said to Inspector James.

"You know what it's like, Sergeant. The enemy within and all that!"

The sergeant did in fact, Rachel thought, look rather dubious. As if he was sure that the code word was bogus and the Inspector was a fake and that he would have them all in custody in no time. Some raggle –taggle bunch of brigands that had something to do with that trouble at the Park. But instead he paled a bit, when the message came through on his radio.

"That was the Chief Constable," he said. "A bit pissed off to be interrupted while he was having his dinner! But he said you are free to go and" – he gulped as he said this – "we are to offer you all possible assistance!"

They drove back towards the outskirts of Cotterham. James had declined the offer of a police escort. Rachel was driving in front with the Inspector, the Transit driven by Carreg was following and Rajma was bringing up the rear in the Land Rover.

"Ice fire!" Rachel said. "Really! That's a code word."

"They've probably got a book somewhere, Rachel," James said, "from which they pluck out such strange combinations. But it has served me well in the past. It's a bit of a door opener!"

Dawn was starting to creep across the sky as they got to the car park of the diner. None of them said much as they went their separate ways; Carreg and Ceridwen in the transit with the fairies and Rajma on her own in the Land Rover. As the two vehicles pulled out, Rajma said:

"See you in London!"

Rachel, Rowena and the Inspector all piled into Rachel's car. They would return to the hotel, get some sleep and then check out. There was no night porter or CCTV and they had a code for the door pad, so no-one would necessarily know they hadn't spent the night there.

Chapter 17

The problem was; what exactly do you do with seven fairies in the middle of London, without causing a public sensation? There was also another, additional problem; how were they going to contact Morgana?

The latter conundrum did not seem to bother the Inspector.

"Don't worry!" He said. "Morgana will contact us!" But Rachel did worry, because time was running out. They had one more day left.

The solution to the first problem wasn't ideal, but they had little choice in the matter; Rajma brought the fairy women to the safe house. She and Carreg had stopped on the way south at a shopping mall and bought clothes for the women and, when they were dressed, divided them between the Land Rover and the Transit van.

One of the fairy women spoke some English, so she travelled with Rajma, along with two of her companions and the other four travelled in the van with Carreg and Ceridwen. The fairy women were a little intimidated by Carreg – Rachel wasn't sure if there was some mutual distrust between their people and his people – so it was necessary to keep Ceridwen on hand. The Transit and the Land Rover staggered their arrivals, so the two groups of thin, pale women, swaddled in coats and hats, didn't look too suspicious.

The flat had four bedrooms and an open plan living area with kitchen attached. It seemed crowded when Rachel arrived; the others had got there first and everything seemed chaotic. But it only had to do for a day and, besides, Rajma and Carreg were going to leave in the morning.

"They've got other jobs to do, Rachel," the Inspector explained. "They can't really be spared any longer."

As usual, he was rather enigmatic and didn't give her any more details. Ceridwen, though, was going to stay. She seemed to have some sort of authority over the women, they deferred to her. When Rachel asked the Inspector about this, he told her:

"Fairies are very hierarchical, Rachel. They can tell she's from a noble family. Actually, they probably know her, or at least know of her, and, whatever they've been told about her, they know they still owe her the respect due her rank."

Things settled down remarkably quickly. Most of the fairy women drifted off to the bedroom to sleep, after they had eaten numerous rounds of buttered toast. It intrigued Rachel; they did not seem to like much of the food that they were offered, but seemed to relish hot, buttered toast smeared with honey and weak tea, without milk, but with plenty of sugar. Ceridwen spent much of the afternoon talking with the women, singly or in pairs, before eventually letting them succumb to sleep.

One of the women lingered in the kitchen. She seemed to be a little older than the others – though who but another fairy could tell the age of a fairy – and seemed almost maternal around them. She was the one who spoke some English.

"You should get some rest," Rachel said to her. "You have been through a lot, you must be exhausted."

Her words sounded trite in light of what the fairy woman had actually endured, but people always fell back on the tried and true phrases, however banal they were.

"And it is not over yet," the woman said, her voice low and subdued. "Because I think you are going to send us back to our people."

Rachel was surprised. Hadn't they been rescuing the women? Wasn't the fairy woman pleased?

"You'll be better – safer – back with your own people, won't you?"

The woman smiled.

"Haf and I left our people because we could not live as we chose. It's true we were tricked into something. We expected to be given jobs, not to become whores. But we left Faerie, because we couldn't live there anymore."

The woman bowed her head, sighed and then said:

"But I am ungrateful! I must apologise to you and say goodnight!"

Rachel had run out of empty words of comfort, so she just wished the woman goodnight.

"By the way," she said. "I'm Rachel."

"My name is Gwyneira," the woman said. "But most people call me Gwyn.

Rachel had made the decision – after discussing it with Inspector James – not to contact her own colleagues. It was well-known that Andy Francis had his sources in the force and in the judiciary, so she didn't want to risk alerting him. She was sure that he already knew what had happened and was taking steps to retrieve the girls, so she didn't want to take any unnecessary chances. She didn't even contact Andrews. It wasn't that she didn't trust her boss, just that she knew that no form of communication was totally secure.

When the fairy women were all asleep – they were all in their various beds by 6pm – the others sat around the living room. At first, they were all quiet and lost in their own thoughts. Rowena was sitting on the sofa next to Ceridwen, cuddled up close. The fairy woman had her arm around the human girl. Carreg was sitting by the window looking out; London and all its people, the constant buzz and bustle of the streets, seemed to fascinate him. Rajma, Rachel and the Inspector were sitting at the table drinking tea.

At last Rajma broke the silence, though almost reluctantly.

"We should eat really," she said. "It's been a long day."

No-one was that hungry - excepting Carreg, who always was - but there were the fairy women to think of, who would probably need more toast before the night was over and had already gone through two loafs of bread and a pot of honey.

"I'll go to the shop and get supplies," Rajma said. And Rachel offered to go with her.

Rachel knew it was a bit of a risk. Her face was known to the Francis clan, but she didn't want Rajma to go on her own, just in case of trouble. Besides, it would give her a chance to be alone with the other woman, as she had questions to ask.

"Ceridwen and Rowena seem close," she said, as they rode the lift down. But Rajma didn't respond, so Rachel put it another way.

"Are they a couple?"

Rajma smiled and answered.

"Not exactly, Rachel. They are very close, it's true. The fairies aren't as rigid as we are about sexuality, so it's often hard to tell the nature of relationships, but I think they are more like very close sisters."

Rachel let it go at that.

The shop was one of those small, stripped-down supermarkets that had virtually replaced the traditional family-run corner shops. Rachel was terrible at shopping. On the occasions when she grudgingly offered to get the groceries, Ellen would give her a list, and even then, she would always forget something.

"You just don't have a shopping mentality!" Ellen would say and Rachel knew what she meant; she just wasn't attuned to it.

Rajma, on the other hand, seemed to be. She effortlessly scooped up supplies for the fairy women – they also seemed to like chocolate and chocolate biscuits, both being akin to a delicacy to them – and a combination of things to "feed the troops", as she put it. They were all snacky things and read-to-eat food, but nobody felt like doing any cooking. Rachel's contribution to shopping was to pick up a few bottles of wine, but when she added to them to the basket, she suddenly realised something. She was sure Rajma was a Muslim.

"Sorry," she said to Rajma, "you don't do you?"

"That's okay," Rajma said. "I don't mind if you do. And by the way I'm tee-total for secular reasons, not religious."

"You'll stick with tea then?" Rachel asked, making a bad joke.

Rajma laughed anyway.

On the way back, they were both quiet and thoughtful. Rachel was thinking of Ellen. She had told her flatmate she would be away from a few days, so she wasn't expected back, but, surprisingly, she was missing the woman. She needed someone to talk to who was sane, ordinary, and not involved in all this bizarre, otherworldly business. It was ironic really, because even if she had been intending to go home, she couldn't really have told Ellen anything about the last few days and, conversely, these recent events were, in fact, the only thing that she really needed to talk about, to get into some perspective.

Rajma abruptly ended Rachel's reverie as they were crossing the square outside the block of flats.

"You'll keep an eye on the Inspector, Rachel, when I'm gone. Won't you?"

"Of course," Rachel said, though she thought the Inspector could probably take care of himself.

"It's just that," Rajma continued, "I think he may have taken on too much, this time."

Rachel asked her what she meant.

"Morgana isn't any ordinary fairy. She's part of a younger generation that are pushing against the bounds of the Treaty and Covenant. She would be delighted if the Inspector was brought down by all this."

Rachel considered this. It had never occurred to her that the Inspector was in any way vulnerable. She said as much.

Rajma smiled.

"There are some on the human side too – those in the know – who would like to see the Treaty broken and swept away. It would suit then if the Inspector was gone. It would be one more obstacle out of the way."

Rachel was about to ask Rajma more questions, but, suddenly, she realised what the niggling sensation that she had started having, just on the edge of her consciousness, actually was. It was that feeling you get when you think you are being watched or followed; almost a physical twinge in the back of your neck.

"Rachel, what is the matter?" Rajma asked.

"Don't stop," Rachel answered. "Just act normally and follow me!"

Rachel walked up the street past the apartment block and took a turn up a cul-de-sac, which led to a development of new houses. At the end of the road was a footpath and, before they turned into it, she paused and stopped, pretending she was taking a phone call. Nobody was following them, it seemed. Or if they were, Rachel thought, they were very good at it.

They walked up the footpath and then quickly took a lane at the back of another set of houses, stopping again where this turned back towards the rear of the apartments. They entered the apartments through the underground car park and made their way up the stairs, eschewing the lifts.

Both of them were red-faced and out of breath, when they got to the flat.

"Were we followed?" Rajma asked.

"I honestly don't know," Rachel answered, "but we should be extra careful."

When the Inspector saw them, he said:

"At last! Glad you are back! Ceridwen was just going to brief us!"

Rachel told him about her suspicions.

"If it's Morgana," Inspector James said, "it saves us the trouble of looking for her. But if it's the Francis gang, that's more worrying. Whoever it is, if it's anyone, we're probably better holed up here than out on the street."

Rachel didn't know if she completely agreed, but this wasn't the time to debate the matter. The fairy women were still asleep and Ceridwen was avid to tell their story before they woke up. Rajma fixed tea and Rachel poured wine. Intriguingly, Carreg also declined the offer of alcohol, preferring tea, but Ceridwen seemed to welcome her glass of wine

The fairy girl was obviously unused to speaking before people and was made uncomfortable by it, but she persevered.

"It was difficult getting all the details from them," she said, "and I don't know what they've been fed with – drugs or alcohol, or a combination of both – but fairies tend to be vague at the best of times and these women are particularly air-headed."

Rachel wondered if that was where the expression "away with the fairies came from", but then realised she was making another bad joke.

"So," Ceridwen continued, "their stories were sometimes unclear about times and places, almost contradictory, but one thing was clear. They weren't actually kidnapped!"

Chapter 18

Sitting in her car later, outside the station, Rachel went over in her mind what Gwyn had briefly told her and what Ceridwen had confirmed later. It had opened up to her a totally new dimension to the affair. From what she had been told, the fairy women – like trafficked women everywhere – had thought they were bound for a better life, better jobs, but had ended up in the sex trade.

That, in itself, was remarkable enough; that the same thing could happen to fairy women that happened to human women. But there was also another aspect to it, which Ceridwen didn't shy away from, to give her her due. Fairies were not supposed to want to leave Faerie. They were supposed to shun humans, keep away from their world and their things, and to even despise them. But these fairy women had thought differently.

Ceridwen had said that they were all servant women or peasant women, the lowest class amongst the fairies and, to them, the human world had seemed more attractive and full of possibilities. That was the problem with the human world, the fairy woman said, it was corrupting and that corruption was contagious.

But, Rachel thought, perhaps it wasn't as simple as Ceridwen seemed to be implying. Gwyn had told her, in the few snippets of conversation that they had snatched, that she and Haf had wanted to leave Faerie, because the human world provided them with the only possibility of a life together. A life that could be lived according to their own rules and not the rules of the fairy aristocracy. Rachel suspected that they were a couple and, however relaxed the fairies were about sexual orientation, for women of their class it wasn't possible to live as a married couple in Faerie.

The revelation added a layer of complication to what had been a simple affair. Morgana's undertaking was not just a straightforward rescue mission – if it was a rescue mission at all – but also a pursuit of runaways. And as Ceridwen well knew, fairy runaways and renegades were at best shunned or and at worst punished.

Rachel looked at her phone. It was 6pm. She figured that all of the day shift would have gone home by now and she was unlikely to run into anybody who might ask her awkward questions or to want something from her. She had parked in the car park at the back of the building. She got out of the car and headed for the back entrance, buzzing herself in.

The office, as she had thought, was deserted. She got some pissed-off looks from the cleaners – she was bound to be in their way – but ignored them and sat at her desk and switched on her PC. She had decided to come into the office because she was fed up with sitting in the flat and just waiting. She had resolved, instead, to do some detective work of her own – that, of course, was what she got paid for - to see if she could track down Morgana. There might be reports of strange sightings or unexplained incidents; anything that could give a hint of the woman's presence out there in the big city.

Thinking of Morgana, as she sat there, she thought of what Ceridwen had said at the end of the briefing.

"I don't know if we should be so quick to give these women back to Morgana. They will be punished for running away, that's certain, the only uncertain thing is the severity of that punishment!"

There had been something of stir then, amongst them, with everyone talking at the same time, but Inspector James had lifted his hands up for silence and said:

"I'm afraid, Ceridwen, it's not up to us to decide. The Treaty and Covenant are clear on this. It's not our decision. We just need to get them back to Morgana, to restore the status quo."

Ceridwen had not been happy with this reply and she had stalked off into one of the bedrooms, followed by Rowena. Carreg had gone back to looking out of the window, withdrawing from the conversation.

"Is that really all we can do?" Rachel had asked.

But neither the Inspector nor Rajma had answered her question.

Andrews had covered her back for the last two days, telling anybody who wanted to know that she was away on assignment, but she had emails waiting for her and various messages, so she knew that it was inevitable that she would have to talk, eventually, to MIT. There was too much to explain, too many bodies piling up. But she wanted it all to be over before she had that conversation. And there only seemed one way in which that was going to happen. However reluctant that she was about agreeing with them, the Inspector and Rajma were right, the women had to go back to Morgana.

Rachel didn't give more than a cursory glance to the emails on her P.C. or the memos on her desk, but there was one message, which she couldn't ignore. It was from Deb. She'd been trying to get hold of Rachel and the tone of the messages was getting more and more desperate. They'd forgotten about Deb. Rachel had thought that Andrews was keeping the channels open -or keeping Deb dangling, whichever way you wanted to put it – and he must have thought that she was the one who was going to do the honours. It crossed her mind that perhaps she should phone Andrews and get him to handle the woman, but it was easier, when all was said and done, to phone her herself.

They agreed to meet in a bar, because where else could you go at that time of night. Deb knew one which was quiet, or so she'd said, though Rachel would have described it another way; expensive and exclusive, more like a club than a pub. She was surprised the door staff let her in, as she was wearing the same jeans and sweater and non-descript coat that she had been virtually living in for the last week. At least I've got clean underwear on she told herself, but didn't want to share this thought with the rather sleek and self-satisfied table staff; all young, pretty and auditioning for some reality TV show that would never get made.

Deb, as always, was immaculately turned out; a symphony in white linen shirt and white jeans, the colour of her clothes a pleasant contrast with her tanned, tight skin and the bronze blond of her hair. She looked dressed for summer. Was it sunny outside, Rachel asked herself, warm even? She hadn't noticed the weather, there was too much else going on.

They didn't do more than acknowledge each other; there were no hugs or warm greetings. Rachel was almost sure now that Deb didn't like her. It was more than the fact that she was a copper and that the Francis clan had an in-built antipathy to the police. It was more a woman-to-woman thing. Deb, Rachel thought, couldn't figure her out, couldn't get a handle on her and consequently she was suspicious of her. It was all, however, papered over with a veneer of politeness, grudging thought it might be.

"How's Donald?" Deb asked, her opening words, and it took Rachel a few moments before she realised who she meant. Andrews was Andrews to her, not Donald.

"He's fine," Rachel said. "Recovering."

As she said it she realised that she didn't actually know how Andrews was and perhaps she should try and find out.

"When I talked to him, he said he was on sick leave. He wouldn't tell me much, but I guess something happened at the exchange."

So, they were in touch, Rachel thought, but she wondered how much Andrews had told her. And was he actually on sick leave or just trying to keep out of Deb's way?

"Did he tell you about what happened?" Rachel asked.

Deb nodded and lowered her head, staring down at her drink.

"He did and Andy said something too."

Deb looked at her, as if waiting for a reaction, as she continued.

"Andy was tamping. In one of his rages!"

Rachel took a sip of her own drink, a very expensive gin and tonic. Artisan gin and artisan tonic, whatever that meant. Just an excuse to push up the prices.

"We didn't get Tony back, but we know that he is okay. And we're working on some other options."

It was hard to pin down exactly what it was that told Rachel – a flicker of Deb's eyes, a twitch of her fingers around the glass, some other slight, subtle movement or gesture – but she was suddenly sure that Deb knew, had always known, what this was all about.

They carried on a desultory conversation, spinning it out, and all the time Rachel was feverishly thinking, looking around her and trying to come up with a plan for getting out of there in one piece. Because it was obvious to her now why Deb had wanted to meet. It wasn't about Tony or Andrews, it was about her.

Andy would have known about the details of their little commando raid, almost as soon as it happened. He would have put her at the scene pretty quickly; she had, for goodness sake, even identified herself as a police officer to one of the security guards. And Andy was angry. Taking a policewoman off the streets of London might be something that he shied away from when sober and calm, but he was neither of these at the moment.

"Look," Deb said, abruptly, "I really need to eat to something. I haven't had anything all day. Shall we get some food? There's a little Greek restaurant around the corner. Family cooking, really good stuff. What do you think?"

It was obvious to Rachel that Deb had overplayed her hand; the invitation to dinner was hurried and bungled, she must be getting desperate. They hadn't been getting on that well. Deb didn't know how to handle women, she was used to batting her eyelashes at men and giving them sweet, little flirty looks, but she lacked the necessary physical vocabulary to do the same with women.

"I don't think so, Deb," Rachel said. "Because we'll never get to the restaurant, will we?"

A look of mock consternation crossed Deb's face.

"And don't even try the little girl lost thing with me. It might work with Andrews – or rather Donald, I should say – but it doesn't work with me. How many of them are waiting for me?"

Deb gave Rachel an appraising look, as if wondering how to play it. But suddenly she relaxed, visibly. The tension that had been in her – only noticeable in its absence – seemed to ease and she sat back in her chair looking Rachel straight in the face.

"Andy made me do it!" She said. "You don't know what he's like!"

Rachel nodded; she thought that she did know.

"The thing is, Deb," she said. "I'm just trying to figure out in my head exactly how many years you would get for being involved in the abduction of a police officer."

There was just a hint of fear on Deb's face now, though she was doing her best to hide it.

"Not just abduction, either, because – let's face it – when they'd got what they wanted out of me, it would be neater for them to make me disappear."

"Andy just wanted a word with you!" Deb said, getting flustered now. "I don't know what you are talking about!"

"One or the other, Deb! You're contradicting yourself!"

Deb stood up to leave, but Rachel barked at her in a voice that even surprised herself.

"Sit down!"

Rachel couldn't figure out how she'd been so stupid that she had walked into this half-asleep. It was so obvious now. And she had nothing on her, no pepper spray or baton. But she knew that they would have been useless anyway. The Francis boys would be armed and they would outnumber her.

"Do you think that I'd have agreed to meet you if I didn't have some sort of back-up plan?" Rachel asked.

Deb looked as if she was considering her answer. Say "no", Rachel urged her mentally, not "yes".

"See, whatever happens, Deb, it's your responsibility! They know I'm meeting you, so whatever happens to me is down to you! They will be coming after you and there's nothing Andy can do to stop them!"

Deb sat stone-faced, considering her options.

"I'm loath to fall back on the stereotypical threats about women's prisons that you always hear on TV, Deb, but you are a good-looking woman!"

Deb didn't know how to take this. It was, in a way, a sort of veiled compliment. But she was a Francis, after all, and used to exercising power, so such pressure didn't work that well on her.

"I'm going to leave now, Detective Sergeant," Deb said.

"That's totally up to you, Deb. I can't detain you. But if you get up from that chair, I can guarantee that Tony will be dead in just over twenty four hours!"

Deb stood up and Rachel thought that she was the one who had overplayed her hand this time. But she didn't leave. Instead, she sat down again.

"There are three men waiting around the corner for us to leave. There is one spotter and two with a van. They are armed!" She said, her voice almost a whisper.

Rachel made the phone call. Urgent back-up needed. Send an ARV. She gave them a few minutes, and then she stood up to go.

"Okay," she said. "Let's get going!"

Deb stood up a little shakily, as if her nerves were shot.

"You don't understand," she said, "Andy won't give up! He knows where you live!"

And that last hackneyed comment was more chilling, more terrifying, that the prospect of the three Francis goons waiting for her outside.

Chapter 19

It was always the case, Rachel thought, just when you were in a hurry and needed to get somewhere, that there was nowhere to park. She spent a few frustrating moments driving around looking for a space, before finding one. Then she left the car at a crazy angle, jumping from it and running as fast as she could towards the flat. She took the stairs three at a time, pounding up them and then burst through her front door.

Ellen was sitting there placidly watching television.

"Oh hullo, Rachel," she said, "I thought you were still away."

Rachel stood there feeling slightly foolish.

"I just got back today!" She said.

The encounter with Andy Francis' men had been more like a scene from a "Carry On" film than an action thriller. Rachel had left the restaurant with Deb, but deliberately lingered by the door as if deep in conversation with the woman. The spotter was sitting in the window of a pub across the road – nice work, if you could get it, Rachel thought – while a black van was parked just up the side street that flanked the restaurant. There really was a Greek restaurant at the end of the road, Rachel noted, and then realised, rather inappropriately considering the circumstances, that she was actually hungry.

The ARV guys phoned her when they were a few minutes out and she directed them to a spot a few yards behind the van, so when she did actually turn the corner with Deb in tow, the two waiting thugs were spread-eagled on the pavement with automatic weapons trained on them, all in a matter of seconds. The spotter, though, got away, and that was why Rachel had made her feverish dash across London.

Ellen wasn't exactly pleased when Rachel told her, in the vaguest of terms, about the threat she was facing.

"I thought you didn't believe in bringing your work home, Rachel!" She said. It was an attempt at humour, but Ellen could never pull off a joke.

When it dawned on Ellen, though, that she was at risk also, by association, she became rather disgruntled, to say the least.

"You should stay home for a couple of day, keep out of circulation. I'll make sure someone is watching the house!" Rachel said.

"I can't take time off, Rachel. You know how things are! Besides, I'd be bored stiff hanging around at home."

"These people are dangerous, Ellen. Ruthless!"

But Ellen was much more perturbed that her daily routine had been upset than fearful. Rachel didn't know whether this was down to her not fully appreciating the danger she was in, or whether it was just Ellen's stubbornness. Whichever it was, she had to admire her bloody-mindedness. In the end, they came up with a compromise. Rachel would drive Ellen to school in the morning – she normally got the bus – and check in with her throughout the day. Rachel had been intending to go back to the safe house that night, but instead she decided to stay home. It wasn't that she thought she could really protect Ellen and herself if Andy Francis truly wanted to take them, but at least she wouldn't have to spend the night worrying about her flatmate.

Just when she had settled down in front of the TV with a glass of wine –her default evening position – her phone rang. It was Andrews.

"I heard, Rachel," he said. "Andy's fucked up this time. He can't get away with it, trying to kidnap an officer off the street!"

Rachel didn't like to point out that, in effect, he had got away with it. There was little to link him to the attempted abduction – his men wouldn't be talking – and Deb would keep schtum, otherwise she'd be incriminating herself. Besides, Rachel had let her go. She had no real reason to hold her or arrest her and she might just be useful out on the street.

"How's the other matter going?" Andrews asked.

"It's progressing, boss," Rachel answered. She knew he wouldn't expect her to go into detail on an unsecured line.

"I think I can keep MIT off your back for a couple of days more, but the proverbial shit will hit the equally proverbial fan by the end of the week."

Putting the phone down, Rachel thought that she was rather sick of people giving her deadlines. Andrews had insisted on posting a car outside the house that night. Rachel had demurred, but was secretly relieved when Andrews insisted. She needed to be able to sleep at least.

Before going to bed, she phoned the safe house. Rajma answered and she told her what had happened.

"I'll be over in the morning, before you leave, just be careful tonight. I'm pretty sure that the Francis gang don't know your location, but I can't be certain!"

There was something about Rajma's voice that put her at ease. Though she wouldn't admit it to herself, she had been scared; more so, in fact, after the event. She could not believe that she had nearly walked into a trap. It would, and she was not exaggerating, have been the end of her. It was that simple. Rajma's voice soothed her, took her away from those dark thoughts.

"I'm aiming to leave about ten, so get here before that," Rajma said. "So, you can say goodbye!"

She said it humorously, but there was warmth in her voice and Rachel needed that warmth at the moment.

"By the way," Rajma continued, "our mutual friends have been in touch. We've organised a meeting tomorrow afternoon. The Inspector will tell you all about it in the morning!"

Rajma's voice was casual and matter-of-fact – just in case someone was listening – but she couldn't completely keep the sense of relief out of it.

Rachel dropped Ellen outside her school in the morning.

"Phone me straight away if you see anything suspicious or out of the ordinary and don't forget to check in with me at break time!"

"Yes, Mum," Ellen said as she slammed the car door shut.

Cheeky bitch, Rachel thought, but she didn't mind, really. As long as Ellen was safe, that was what mattered. At least Rachel got paid for being in the line of fire, Ellen didn't, and Rachel felt bad about getting her involved.

She got to the safe house just before 10am – the traffic had been particularly bad that morning and Rajma and Carreg were on the point of departure. Though there was the usual round of good wishes, handshakes and hugs, which accompanied farewells, there was no disguising the tense atmosphere which hung over the flat. Rachel walked Rajma out to the Land Rover, an excuse to find out what was happening.

"The women have got wind, somehow, of what the Inspector intends to do. I think they are afraid; fearful of what Morgana might do to them. As we said, they are runaways, and the fairies take a dim view of such behaviour."

The Land Rover was parked in the underground car park – each flat had two parking spaces, a luxury in that part of the capital – and as Carreg loaded their bags, Rachel asked Rajma how Morgana had made contact.

"Basically, the Inspector went and hung out in the pub across the road. The place you were taken from. He figured out that Morgana would keep a watch on the place and he was right. She met him there and they made an arrangement."

Then it was time for Rajma to go and the two women hugged. And it wasn't one of those perfunctory, social hugs. Rachel had grown really fond of the young woman. And Rachel wasn't the sort to make friends easily. Her school reports had always said "doesn't play well with others" or "socially isolated", as if she was some sort of freak, while, all the time, the truth was that she just didn't like half the kids she had to mix with every day. So, when Rachel found a friend, it was a rare occasion and something to be treasured.

"I hope we run into each other again," Rajma said. And then as an after-thought. "Come down and visit us again in Abermannan!"

"I will!" Rachel said and she meant it.

Chapter 20

Rachel sat in her car with the Inspector, watching the tree line. She should be feeling, she thought, some sense of accomplishment or completion, because the whole affair was nearly over. They were due to make the exchange within the hour. Ceridwen was parked back at the visitor centre in the Transit, just awaiting their call, and the fairy women, though frightened, were subdued and resigned to their fate. Once this was over with, Rachel though, she could go back to the mundane world of ordinary, natural policing. She'd have loose ends to tie up, it was true, stories to tell, people to convince – MIT being her major headache – but then her life could resume. She'd welcome the boredom of the mundane after this.

She'd only been to Epping Forest a couple of times before – joyless walks with her ex-husband and the dog that she'd paid for and he'd kept – so her memories of it weren't exactly fond. She thought of it as a sort of joyless green waste, a place for assignations and for lost souls. A very apt location, she considered, for what they were about.

She knew that she should have felt some sort of professional satisfaction in concluding matters, but instead the whole affair just left a bad taste in her mouth. She wondered if, instead of rescuing the fairy women, they were just delivering them back to a life of drudgery or virtual slavery.

She had been over it time and again with the Inspector, but it had always come back to the same thing.

"These women are not under our jurisdiction," Inspector James would say. "Our laws have no relevance in the matter. They are not citizens of this country, they are subjects of Faerie."

"But don't they have any rights? Any say in what happens to them?"

"Not in the same way that we have – or think we have – Rachel. The Treaty and Covenant allows for two different systems living in parallel to each other. You could say, though, that we occupy the same space, but not the same time-frame. Putting it crudely, for Faerie, the Enlightenment never happened, so they have no concept of individual rights. They basically run a sort of medieval society, based on feudal bonds between masters and servants. We may not like it, but it's not our right to judge it or interfere with it."

Now they sat in silence waiting on the side of a dirt track, just inside the forest. Time went by in excruciatingly small degrees; Rachel kept looking at her phone, but the minutes dragged on and the only sense of the afternoon passing was the softening of the light and the sun slowly slipping down the sky.

"They are not coming," the Inspector said.

"Perhaps Morgana is delayed," Rachel answered. "Or perhaps we are in the wrong place?"

"No. This was the place they meant. I'm sure of it! Something's gone wrong."

She phoned Ceridwen to tell her that the exchange was off and that they were coming back. The fairy woman was outside the Transit when they drew up in the visitor centre car park and she didn't look too pleased.

"What's happened?" She asked. "They're getting restless in the back and we're starting to get looks! I've tried shutting them up, but they're either crying or complaining!"

"I've no idea what's happened, Ceridwen," the Inspector said, almost brusque for once. "We'd better get back to the safe house."

It was past nine o'clock when Rachel left the apartment. The fairy women were either catatonic or hysterical and it was all Ceridwen could do to keep them under control. She had scolded them, threatened them – or at least that's what Rachel thought she was doing, the shouting was all in fairy – and eventually they seemed to subside. Meanwhile, the Inspector was making a series of telephone calls. He just waved vaguely to her as she left.

She was mentally and physically exhausted and felt the need to get away. To get home and get some sleep. She realised that she had keyed herself up - using reserves of strength that she didn't know she had - that afternoon and the disappointment, the anti-climax, had drained her of any energy she had left.

She parked her car on the street and nodded to the two officers in the squad car posted outside the flat. She'd been hoping that this would be over too; she knew that the surveillance was a necessity, but she just didn't like the idea of being watched all the time.

She opened the door to the flat and put her keys down on the table in the hall, as she always did.

"Hi, Ellen," she shouted out, but got no response. Looking through the doorway of the sitting room she could see that her flatmate was sitting on the sofa, with the TV on, and, by the look of it, she'd fallen asleep. Rachel sighed. She'd wanted company, just a normal conversation, but she couldn't really wake Ellen up. Instead she went into the kitchen to see what was in the fridge and, being disappointed by the lack of anything easy or appetising, she thought again and went into the living room, her eyes on the open bottle of red wine on the coffee table.

She didn't know, afterwards, how she had sensed the other presence in the room; perhaps she'd subconsciously picked up a noise, a rustle, the sound of breathing. Or perhaps there was some disturbance in the air, the aura of the place. Whatever it was, she was not surprised, when a voice said:

"Welcome home, Rachel!"

Morgana stood up from the chair behind the door where she had been sitting and moved towards her, hands outstretched. Rachel knew what she intended to do and, as Morgana came closer, she batted the woman's right arm away with her own left arm and punched her in the stomach with her right hand.

"Ow!" Morgana said, as Rachel's hand caught her in the gut, and Rachel echoed the sound. She felt that she'd broken her hand. She hadn't realised that the fairy woman was still wearing a cuirass under her outer garment. As Rachel flinched, in pain, Morgana put her hand on Rachel's face, trying to put a glamour on her.

But Rachel fought it. The Inspector had said that it was a question of will power. Hers against Morgana's. She'd seen the maid at Dunstan Park nearly fight off Ceridwen's attempt to glamour her, so she knew it could be done. It was like hypnotism, she told herself, the trick was being unreceptive.

Morgana's right hand, as it touched Rachel's face sent a warm shock – an almost electric burst of energy – through first her jaw and then, diffusing out, upwards towards the top of her head, her consciousness. It wasn't painful; rather it was soothing and she so wanted to surrender to it, to sweet rest and sleep. She closed her eyes, on the point of giving in, but then marshalled one last rebellious effort and, drawing back her battered hand, suddenly slapped Morgana across the face.

"Fuck! You bitch!" Morgana cried out, in very unfairy-like language, but she withdrew her hand, reaching towards the dagger at her belt. Rachel grabbed her arms and they fell forwards into the hall. Morgana was smaller than Rachel, lighter, but her hands and arms were hard and sinewy. She was much stronger than she looked and, in seconds, she was out from under Rachel and their positions were reversed. Morgana put her knees on Rachel's chest. Rachel struggled, until she felt the blade of the dagger against her throat and then she stopped. Then, through the bad dream of terror and pain, the effort of getting her breath back and trying not to scream out, she heard a sound that was strangely out of place. Morgana was laughing.

"Where did you learn to resist a glamour?" She asked.

"Where did you get my address?" Rachel countered with her own question.

"Where do you think?" Morgana replied. "You were my prisoner."

Of course, Rachel thought, of course she would know. They'd been through her bag, when she was their prisoner.

"What have you done to Ellen?"

"You know what I've done to her, Rachel. She'll be alright. She's just having a pleasant dream"

"A nightmare more like!" Rachel spat the words out, but then felt the blade cut into her throat.

"Careful, Rachel!" Morgana said. "I have an urge to shed human blood today, so don't make it yours!"

"Just tell me what you want!"

"I want to know who betrayed me," Morgana said.

"I have no idea what you are talking about!"

As Rachel said the words, Morgana's face – hovering as it was a few inches from Rachel's face – seemed to grow even more savage. She opened her mouth and showed those small, pointed teeth that seemed to be common trait of fairy women. At another time, in another circumstance, they might even have looked rather cute.

Christ, she's not going to bite me, is she? Rachel thought. She felt the dagger press harder, but then, suddenly, the hand holding it relaxed and the face lost its savage sheen, dissolving into a grim sort of smile.

"I think you are telling the truth," Morgana said. "You wouldn't dare lie to me!"

It was Rachel's turn to laugh, though the sound that came out of her mouth was more of strangled grunt than anything else.

Morgana pressed the blade harder against Rachel's throat.

"As long as I live, I will never understand humans! Why are you laughing? You should be begging for mercy!"

Morgana realised that Rachel couldn't actually speak with the blade pressed against her, so she relented and released the pressure.

"Now tell me what you find so funny!"

"Let me sit up first!" Rachel said.

"You can sit, but not stand," Morgana said, getting off her. Rachel had noticed that the woman had her own scent – spicy and heady – and wasn't sure if she actually smelt like that naturally or was wearing some sort of perfume. Perhaps fairies had their own equivalent of Chanel No. 5. Or perhaps it was Chanel No.5!

"Don't try anything, Rachel! Don't shout out or attack me! I could slit your little friend's throat in the blink of a human eye."

"She's done nothing to you!" Rachel said, easing her back up against the kitchen units. "She's just an innocent bystander!"

Morgana smiled at her again, that strange cat-like expression that had no mercy in it.

"That's the trouble with you humans, Rachel," Morgana said. "You are a strange mixture of savagery and sentimentality. And you are hardly innocent, any of you!"

Morgana sighed, as if she, too, was tired. Well, Rachel thought, I suppose fairies have bad days as well as humans.

"No! I wouldn't slit your friend's throat to be cruel. I would do it because I said I would! Now, anyway, tell me why you were laughing!"

"I was laughing at you because you are so self-assured," Rachel took a breath before she said the next words, after all Morgana was armed and definitely dangerous, "and, quite frankly, arrogant. Though, of course, that's not surprising."

"Why is it not surprising?" Morgana asked, seemingly intrigued by Rachel's words.

"Well, I suppose it's the whole princess thing. The sense of entitlement. Always getting your own way."

Morgana looked at Rachel. Like a cat looking at a mouse, Rachel thought, that's where I've seen that expression. Then suddenly it was her turn to laugh.

"You do amuse me, Rachel! I really should take you back with me! The things you say!"

"Well, Princess, or whatever I'm supposed to call you." Rachel said. "As you know that I'm not going to try anything stupid, can I pour myself a glass of wine? I'm dying for a drink!"

She stood up and Morgana made no move to stop her. She got a glass out of the cabinet and then, as a second thought, took another one.

"Wine?" She asked. Morgana nodded and moved to the sofa, sitting next to Ellen.

"Thank you!" The fairy said. "You can call me Morgana, by the way, you're not one of my subjects."

She took the wine and sipped it, but didn't comment, then turned to face Ellen.

"Is this one your servant or your paramour?"

"Flat-mate!" Rachel answered and Morgana laughed again.

"Oh, what quaint little lives you humans lead!"

Chapter 21

Morgana led the way down to the basement of the building and then further. They took a service elevator to a sub-basement that Rachel had not previously known existed and then followed a low tunnel – as sort of service conduit, Rachel thought – to what looked to be a blank wall. But just past the blank wall was a niche tucked away in a hidden corner and in the niche was a trap door. It could have been a drain cover or the seal on an ancient well, but, to those who knew, like Morgana, it was the entrance to another world below the capital.

When they were both below the trap door, Morgana lit a lantern that she found hanging on a sconce on the wall and started climbing down a metal ladder that was attached to the side of a downward shaft. As Rachel followed she asked herself, not for the first time:

"What the hell am I doing here?"

Their conversation in the flat, over the glasses of wine, had been remarkably civilised, considering the way it had started, with a dagger at Rachel's throat. Morgana told Rachel that the Cimbriani had arrived in Epping Forest early in the afternoon of that day to make the exchange. They had driven out there in two vehicles – she was vague about the detail, cars not being a fairy thing – and had left Tony Francis in one of them with two guards. Then she had set off into the forest with six companions to scout out the rendezvous point. But they had never made it. They had been ambushed on the way.

"They must have known exactly where we were heading, Rachel," Morgana said. "Because my people never get taken unawares like that. Or somebody must have betrayed our presence!"

One of her companions had been killed in the first burst of fire and two wounded. The survivors had managed to get away – melting into the undergrowth, the way that fairies could – but she had had to leave the body of their dead comrade. When they returned to the other car, Tony Francis was gone and one of his guards dead, the other severely wounded.

"We never leave our dead, Rachel," she said and seemed, for once, genuinely upset, "it is a great dishonour!"

Rachel had noticed that Morgana had quite a thirst for wine and also the capacity to drink it. She'd had a few glasses, but didn't seem drunk, just slightly mellower. More human, Rachel thought, if that's possible.

"And so you thought the Inspector had betrayed you?" Rachel asked.

"Humans are perfidious, Rachel! I'd expect nothing else from them."

"There is another explanation," Rachel said. "A more likely one, because how could we have known exactly which route you would take to the rendezvous?"

Morgana was watching her now, a keen look in her eyes. Rachel hesitated, but Morgana urged her on.

"Say what you have to say! I'm all ears, as you humans put it, which is an apt, if ludicrous, expression!"

"Did it not occur to you that one of your own people could have betrayed you?"

Morgana looked fierce again.

"Never!" She spat out.

"You know of Ceridwen? The fairy woman who works with the Inspector?"

"The renegade, you mean," Morgana said and looked as if she was about to spit again.

Rachel persevered.

"Ceridwen talked to some of the captive fairy women. It appears that they were not so much kidnapped as tricked into becoming prostitutes. They thought they were going to legitimate jobs."

It suddenly occurred to Rachel that Morgana knew this already; she didn't show any signs of shock or surprise, just slightly narrowing her eyes as if thinking.

"What is your point, Rachel? What are you trying to say? None of my people would dare betray me!"

"But somebody did! Somewhere along the line!"

"The person you are talking about paid for his treachery with his life, though we didn't kill him ourselves. His body was returned to our homeland."

That was the body in the morgue, Rachel thought.

"Perhaps there are others? Perhaps someone was in league with him?"

Morgana would not admit to the possibility and told Rachel that she was talking nonsense.

"It doesn't change things, Morgana," Rachel said, trying to rack her brains for a way out of the mess she was in, "not really."

"How so?" Morgana said, looking rather archly at Rachel as she asked the question. "I have lost the goods I had to trade. Though..." - and here she paused and smiled at Rachel, showing her pointed teeth – "…. I do have you now, of course."

There was something particularly chilling about Morgana's smile, Rachel thought, that cat contemplating mouse thing again. And Rachel, of course, was the mouse.

"The Inspector will return the girls to you, anyway. He's doing it because of the Treaty, not because of Tony Francis."

"If you give me your word, Rachel, swear it, I will believe you."

Morgana paused before she went on:

"But be warned, don't give your oath idly to the Fair Folk, because we will hold you by your words. And you will be coming with me to seal the deal!"

On the way out, Rachel stopped to have a word with the two officers in the squad car. The sort of jokey banter that passed for conversation in the force.

"Out on a job!" She told them. "No rest for the wicked!"

She had no more idea of how Morgana had got out of the flat without being seen than she had of how the woman had got in, in the first place, but as she walked to her car, the fairy princess suddenly appeared besides her.

"I woke your friend up," she said. "Told her she was tired and needed to go to bed! She'll think that she dreamt me in the morning."

Morgana was wearing jeans and zipped top of some sort – a sporty looking thing, which was loose enough to hide her cuirass and her dagger. She had popped a woollen hat over her head to hide her ears, but even dressed like this, she looked gorgeous. Her beauty – ethereal and fragile as it was – could not be totally diminished by her drab surroundings or her anonymous clothes.

"Where's your sword?" Rachel asked, to distract herself from the strange attraction she was feeling towards the woman. The Inspector had told her that a fairy princess like Morgana would have an almost tangible charisma that was hard to resist, but she hadn't really believed him until now.

"I don't wear it when I take the Tube," Morgana answered. "It gets tangled up in people's legs."

Rachel laughed, but then realised that Morgana wasn't trying to make a joke.

Morgana was a reluctant passenger. Fairies didn't seem to like cars, though they would, at a pinch, make use of them. When Rachel made a comment about this, Morgan answered:

"Where would you rather be, Rachel? Riding a horse over a mountainside in the moonlight, or stuck in this smelly, polluting machine?"

Rachel's car wasn't that smelly, but she understood the sentiment.

Rachel had phoned Inspector James before leaving the flat.

"There's a mutual acquaintance of yours here," she had said. "And she wants to get the deal we discussed done!"

Rachel had to explain that the 'package' they were expecting, was missing. She'd told Morgana that this wasn't necessarily a problem and hoped that she hadn't promised what she couldn't deliver. The Inspector paused on the other end and Rachel thought she was going to have to spell it all out in no uncertain terms. But eventually, as she was almost sure he would, he said:

"We can do it anyway. Arrange a time and place. I'll wait for your message."

That was the easy part; the hard part was when Morgana still insisted that Rachel go with her.

"A mark of your good faith, Rachel! Just to prove that you didn't betray us! Then we will set up a meeting tomorrow, together!"

So that was why Rachel found herself driving along with Morgana in the night heading for London University's Senate House.

"We had to go deep under, Rachel!" Was all that Morgana would say. "And that is the closest way in and back to my people!"

Morgana seemed to be able to walk into buildings, past security staff and through locked doors with ease. Senate House was no exception; it was closed and locked up, but Morgana led them to a side entrance, which she opened without difficulty.

On the ladder now, staring down at the figure disappearing into the shadows below her, Rachel suddenly felt panicked. What if this had all been a ruse on Morgana's part, she asked herself, what if the woman had led her here to imprison her again? But then they were at the bottom of the ladder and, passing through a low doorway, they entered a series of ancient tunnels and Rachel was too intrigued by her surroundings to feel very afraid.

The tunnels looked as if they had been cut from the rock and, in places, pillars and doorways of stone had been constructed, where sections branched off. Morgana moved forward in front of her carrying another lantern she had taken from the chamber at the bottom of the shaft. Like the first one, which she had left, with surprising consideration, in the shaft, it was just a small, glassed-in sphere with a hook on top, holding a candle, so the light was faint, but, anyway, fairy eyes were better than human ones in the dark.

"Where are we?" Rachel asked in wonder.

Morgana stopped, turned towards her and smiled.

"You are deep under your city, where human feet have seldom trod. You are now in the realm of Faerie!"

"But when was all this built?" Rachel asked.

"A thousand years ago or more! Because once, Rachel, fairies and humans lived together in harmony up there above us! It may be hard to believe, but it's true!"

It did seem incredible to Rachel, unbelievable as Morgana had said.

"Oh, we were never that close," Morgana continued. "There was always an element of separation. Mutual superstition you could call it. But a sort of harmony, none the less."

Morgana held the lantern up to the walls, moving along them and circling back. In the light Rachel could see that the walls were coloured in places with frescos, scenes of humans and animals and – yes, it definitely was – fairies!

"Then the Romans came and the Saxons and we retreated to the forests and the wild places. But here in this city, this ancient place, which was as fairy as it was human, we would not leave. We went underground, we went deep enough so that no-one could find us, could seek us out. These were our places of refuge."

Morgana seemed suddenly happy, almost childlike.

"Come along now!" She said. "You must see this!"

And she led Rachel on down the tunnel.

Soon they came to a wide arched doorway and beyond it into a cavernous space. As Morgana held her lantern high, Rachel could see that they were in a columned hall, a magnificent high, lofty chamber. The ceilings, pillars and walls were ornately carved with sculptures and decorations; animal figures, fairy warriors, trees and leaves.

"This was a palace, Rachel! Finer than any building above, out there in the world beyond!"

"But what happened to these people?" Rachel asked. "Where did they go?"

It was obvious to her that the tunnels - this whole complex of rooms, chambers and palaces - were long abandoned; nothing remained except echoes, shadows of the people who had lived here.

"No-one knows," Morgana said, her voice now filled with sorrow. "They left or died or just disappeared. Living underground, hiding, is not the sort of life that appeals to my people. Our palaces may be under the earth, but our hearts and souls are out there riding on the wind. Without that, these people could no longer exist here."

They were both subdued after this, lapsing into silence. Morgana led them on, down endless corridors, until they turned a corner and came to a doorway. The door itself was solid – oak, Rachel thought – studded with iron, as if built for defence. Morgana knocked on it – several times – and eventually it was opened. The fairy warrior, who opened it bowed his head to Morgana and then glared at Rachel. Morgana said something and he moved aside to let them in.

They were in a lighted chamber, with a hearth and chimney at one end of the room. I wonder where the smoke goes, Rachel thought, but then decided that people who could build such elaborate underground architecture would have figured that out. Looking around her, she realised that she was in what could have been described as a courtyard, as there were stairs and balconies leading to individual rooms that lined three of the walls of the place. The ceiling was so high that it was in darkness, the light from the fire and the lanterns around the walls not penetrating that far.

"As I said, Rachel," Morgana turned to her as she spoke, "we have gone deep. No-one will find us here!"

It was a strange place to sleep, but sleep she did. She was exhausted after all and, truth be told, a little overwhelmed. It was as if she was in a waking dream. Though Morgana insisted that she drink and eat something before bed – the fairies were hospitable, good hosts to their guests - she retired as soon she could, to a chamber on the upper tier of rooms that she was to share with Morgana.

The bed chamber was furnished with two platforms that had been cut from the rock, like little cubby-holes Rachel thought, lined with mattresses and quilts; soft, lineny things of a fine sort of workmanship that she had never seen before. You don't buy sheets like this in Tesco, Rachel thought. More material, fine and gauzy this time, had been placed as a curtain over the doorway, where the remains of an old, rotten door, still clung in places to the brickwork.

"You can sleep safely here, Rachel." Morgana said. "You are under my protection and no-one will hurt you."

Fairies, Rachel noticed, went to sleep silently and quickly, lying on their backs – or at least Morgana did – whereas Rachel tossed and turned and thought that she would never get off. But she did eventually. And then it seemed only minutes before someone was waking her.

To her surprise, it wasn't Morgana, but a thin, frail teenage girl, in a dress of some sort, with a scarf tied around her head holding in her hair. With a shock, Rachel realised that the girl was human, though her skin was as pale and smooth as a fairy's and her eyes, not fairy-green but blue and deep as the ocean, had that same faraway look.

"Come!" The girl said in unsure, unsteady, English. "The Princess waits for you!"

The girl led the way down the stairs and towards the hearth, where Morgana was seated on a stool before a table, while her people bustled around her at various tasks.

"Thank you, Elis!" Morgana said and the girl smiled and sat down in front of the princess on the floor of the chamber.

"Good morning, Rachel!" Morgana continued. "Today I hope that we will finish this business, so I can go home! There is food and drink here for you to break your fast!"

There was a sort of white cheese and little cakes that seemed to be flavoured with honey. There was also a sweet drink in a jug, which Rachel thought was mead. Obviously, Rachel mused, fairies had a taste for sweet things.

"No tea or coffee, I'm afraid Rachel. We never got the taste for those, like your people did. Of course, we never went out and conquered other people's lands, which probably accounts for that!"

Morgana sighed and looked around her. She seemed out of sorts this morning, jaded or fatigued.

"I'd sorely like to get out of this city," she said. "I brought a war band of fifteen warriors to London. I go home with three of my comrades dead and five wounded. It was perhaps too great a price to pay!"

"Have you thought more on what I said?" Rachel asked, but Morgana looked at her perplexed. "It could be one of these people – one of your warriors that betrayed you – you should take care."

"That cannot be, Rachel. My people are loyal."

Rachel didn't want to pursue the matter further, so she changed the subject.

"The girl," she said, nodding at Elis. "She's human!"

Elis was leaning against Morgana, her head on her lap. The fairy was stroking the girl's head.

"What of it?" Morgana asked. "She has been with me for years, since she was a little creature."

"Shouldn't she be back with her own people?"

"I am her people, Rachel. Not all human children are wanted you know! This child was hungry, hurt, terrified. She isn't any longer! She is loved and cherished!"

Rachel didn't want to push things further, so she shut up, but Elis gave her what could only be described as a filthy look.

The fairies were a surly and odd-looking lot, mostly male, though there were two females amongst them. They were all dressed in various combinations of human clothes, so that they could pass among people on the streets, but were all carrying swords or long daggers, armed also with bows or crossbows. They either ignored Rachel, or glared at her, but one of the women, a girl with ashen, blond hair and a fetching smile, said something in fairy to Morgana, which made her laugh.

"Rhian is asking if you're my prisoner and, if so, whether she can buy you off me."

Rachel felt just an inkling of concern; she sincerely hoped that there hadn't been a misunderstanding and that Morgana didn't think that she really was her prisoner.

"I told her that you would cost at least two horses, or five of her white cattle!"

The vague concern that Rachel felt turned suddenly to alarm. But seeing the expression on her face, Morgana laughed:

"I'm joking! I told her that you were our ally now, which I hope is true."

Morgana gave Rachel a long, steady look. It was a warning of sorts.

"Rhian is my second in command, but she only speaks a little English. She can also manage Welsh, but I suppose that's not very helpful for you. But we should tell her what's happening."

So, they sat, with Morgana translating. But discussing possible plans with fairies was a frustrating business. The conversation went round and round in circles. In the end they finally agreed that they would set a time for the meeting with Inspector James. The location was more difficult. Morgana, still suspicious, wanted a place of her own choosing with plenty of woodland to cover her people. Rhian said something and Morgana translated.

"Rhian says that she has heard that there is a wondrous place called Burnham Beeches to the west of this city. It is meant to be very beautiful, a place with much of the spirit about it."

Rachel wasn't sure if Morgana was making another joke, but then realised that she was deadly serious. Rachel vaguely remembered Burnham Beeches, thought it was a pleasant place, but no spiritual Nirvana.

"We should meet in the late afternoon, when there are not many people about and to give us time to get there," Rachel said, presuming the fairies had transport. "I'll phone the Inspector as soon as we get out of here."

She had to explain to them that her mobile would not work underground. Rhian said something.

"What did she say?" Rachel asked Morgana.

Fairies, Rachel had noticed, tended not to lie or dissemble. Morgana had made no attempt to mislead her. The fact that Rachel knew nothing about the Inspector's wife was irrelevant to them. Rachel remembered the figure she had seen on the stairs in James' house. Was that his wife? She'd almost thought it was a trick of the light or something she'd dreamed. Anyway, she told herself, she couldn't think about that now, there were more pressing matters.

"One more thing," Rachel said. "Keep the time and location of the meeting secret from your warriors!"

Neither Morgana nor Rhian had liked it, but they had agreed in the end. Treachery to them was an unforgivable crime and suspecting someone of it was nearly as bad as the act itself. Humans, they knew, were perfidious, but not fairies!

Though on the face of it, the fairy camp seemed chaotic and disorganised, the fairies with a surprising turn of speed and an unsuspected efficiency, packed up, cleared up and were ready to go within the hour.

The party that set out totalled twelve. There were nine warriors, including Rhian, two of these wounded in some way – Rachel had been told by Morgana that the bodies of the dead fairies had been transported back to their homeland, by the other wounded fairies – plus Morgana, Elis and Rachel. Seeing how depleted the warrior band was, it was clear to Rachel that, though the fairies were fierce warriors and had a particular talent for stealth and surprise, they were ultimately no match for the firepower of the Francis clan or the sheer number of thugs that Andy could call upon if pressed. They were a people from another age, out of time and out of sync with the modern world.

The journey back took them by a different route, even deeper. They left the palace level that they had been on and took to steps that led downwards, until the steps ran out and they then followed a tunnel that sloped upwards. The fairies kept a tight, disciplined order, with scouts out front and a rearguard behind. This puzzled Rachel somewhat, as she thought that they could not be in any danger from Andy Francis, lost this deep underground.

Suddenly, just as Rachel was starting to feel more and more disquieted, the whole party stopped at a signal from one of the scouts. Rachel could see the breath of the fairies steaming in the cold air, in the light of the lanterns they held. Their faces were set and attentive, eyes looking around them at the dark shadows of the walls, ears straining for any noise. She noticed that Elis had moved right up besides Morgana and that the princess had put her arms around the girl, as if to comfort her.

What the hell is happening? Rachel asked herself, but then she heard the noise. It was like an animal was there somewhere ahead of them; there was a definite snuffling noise and the rattle of something – claws perhaps – against the walls. A chill fear washed over her, a panic that threatened to overwhelm her. It was the most visceral of terrors; she was lost in the dark, in a confined place with some creature hunting her. She did all she could to master herself, suppress the fear. She wondered, trying to think rationally and clearly, whether the fairies had more acute hearing than she had, whether they'd heard these noises before her and that's why they had stopped.

The noises seemed to subside, then abruptly stop. On a hand signal from Morgana they moved forward again in silence. There were one or two more stops as they heard noises again – or imagined they did – but eventually – it seemed like an age had passed, but it was actually just over an hour – they came to the bottom of a shaft and started ascending a series of steps cut into the sides. Then they passed through a gate – a rusted metal grille of ancient design – and through another low shaft into what Rachel recognised as a disused Tube tunnel leading to a station, marooned in time, all art deco design and aging posters advertising Beechams Salts and Five Boys Chocolate.

The fairies were visibly more relaxed now and had started talking again, whispering to each other. Rhian, who seemed to act as the sergeant-major, while Morgana was definitely officer class, let them carry on chatting, only occasionally shushing them, when they came to a bend or a branch in the tunnel.

"What was that, down there?" Rachel asked Morgana, when they had stopped for a brief rest and to send scouts ahead, the very act of enquiring bringing back a residual, cold wash of fear.

Morgana looked at Rachel for a few moments as if unwilling to answer or unsure of what she was going to say.

"There are other things living underground, Rachel, not just my people. Better not to ask too many questions about them, you may not like the answers!"

And that was all she would say.

They came out of a shaft into the open air through a manhole tunnel. The last hundred yards or so had been up an iron-runged ladder, so Rachel was feeling the results of the exertion. She was, after all, a runner not a climber. They had emerged on a building plot, land that had been cleared and fenced in, ripe for re-development as expensive, designer apartments destined for some off-shore landlord. Rachel wondered how the fairies navigated underground; they didn't appear to have maps, but seemed to know the route, and this was obviously the place they had aimed for, as their vehicles were parked, hidden by hoardings, at one angle of the fence.

Though the fairies didn't show any fatigue – although Elis looked as tired as Rachel – they all sat for a few moments of rest on the ground by the man-hole cover in the sun, which was warm and welcome after the gloom of the underworld. That was when Rachel heard it, the text alert. She reached for her phone, only then remembering that she'd turned it off to save the battery. She didn't think anything of it, at first, but then it suddenly struck her. One of the fairies had a mobile phone.

So what? She thought. It doesn't necessarily signify anything. They seem to have readily adapted in some ways to our world, so why not phones?

But then she decided to tell Morgana.

There was no drama involved, no searching people or getting them to turn their bags out. In the end, the fairy who had the phone gave it up voluntarily, when Rhian asked. Or so it seemed to Rachel who didn't actually understand any of the exchange of words that was going on. Rhian gave the phone to Rachel.

"You understand these things, Rachel," Morgana said. "What can you tell from it?"

Very little, as it turned out. The text that had been received was just a question mark. There were no named contacts or numbers and all outgoing and ingoing messages had been deleted. But this – all these deletions – was suspicious in itself.

"I can't prove it," Rachel told Morgana, "but this could explain why your location was betrayed and you were ambushed."

Morgana didn't exactly seem pleased by the information and Rhian, when the princess had translated, seemed overtly hostile. They walked off some way and whispered together furiously. The fairy, who had surrendered the phone, was sitting on his own on an upturned cable drum, his face inscrutable, but, seeing Rachel's gaze on him, he briefly glared at her, before returning his eyes to the middle distance again.

"It is a grave concern to them," a voice said and Rachel almost recoiled in surprise. The girl, Elis, had suddenly appeared beside her and was talking to her in a low, reedy voice, almost a whisper. "Fairies do not betray each other, especially if they have sworn an oath like Gerallt has."

Elis had not spoken to Rachel before, unless prompted, and then in very halting English, so now she appeared almost garrulous.

"They are discussing what to do."

Elis suddenly grew quiet and then sidled away. Morgana and Rhian were returning. They walked up to Gerallt, who, unprompted, fell on his knees before the princess. There was an exchange of words – cold ones from Morgana, angry ones from Rhian and monosyllables from Gerallt – and then it seemed to be settled. The fairies all moved off to the vehicles.

"You must make your phone call, Rachel," Morgana, now at her side, said. "Arrange the meeting!"

"What are you going to do with Gerallt?" Rachel asked.

Morgana seemed to grow angry at the question.

"It is none of your concern!"

"You won't kill him!" Rachel blurted out, she had seen how quick to anger the fairies were.

Morgana gave a mirthless chuckle.

"There are too few of us to start killing each other. We are not as numerous as you humans! Gerallt will atone for his crime in battle or in exile. He will take his chances."

It did not take long to set up the meeting, Rachel brushed aside the Inspector's concerns – yes, of course she was alright, yes, they hadn't harmed her in any way – and rang off.

She told Morgana the details, expecting that to be an end to it, hoping that she could walk away. But it wasn't going to be that easy.

"You are staying with me, Rachel!" The princess insisted. "We'll see this through together! Finally finish it!"

Chapter 22

The meeting - or exchange, if you could call it that - was a low-key event, almost an anti-climax. Rachel sat in her car in the visitors' car park just off the main common of Burnham Beeches. Though Morgana hadn't said as much, it was obvious to Rachel that the princess trusted Inspector James and didn't expect any treachery. Reluctant, as she had been to accept it at first, Morgana had recognised the truth of Gerallt's guilt, that much was obvious.

Rachel had insisted that they pick her car up on the way. She'd left it near Senate House and she didn't want it clamped and towed away. It was all very well dealing with fairies and gang wars, but you also had to take care of the mundane, little details of life. Morgana, though, would not leave her side until the trade was completed, so they drove out of town together, taking a different route from the other fairies, who were divided up between a beat-up Ford Mondeo, a mini-bus and an old Rover saloon. Rachel wondered where the fairies got their cars – some dubious car dealer in the wilds of Cumbria, she supposed – and thought that they'd probably been ripped off.

Elis was loath to leave Morgana and clung onto her; she was going with one of the other parties. Morgana petted her, said some soft words, but eventually spoke harshly to her. The girl left in floods of tears.

"You see," she said in explanation, "human children get attached to us. We are not as cruel as you think!"

Rachel had never thought that the fairies were particularly cruel – just very other – but she thought that Morgana was, in fact, articulating what she thought humans believed; fairies were mysterious and magnificent, but cruel and heartless too.

It was strange to be sitting in the car with Morgana on their own and car travel tends to elicit conversation from even the most taciturn of people. Something to do, Rachel thought, with the fact that you are both staring in front of you, not looking at each other.

As they passed through the streets and the traffic, the whole hustle and bustle of the capital around them, flowing over them, Morgana suddenly said:

"There are so many of you, like ants, and always as busy as they are; making things, selling things, spending your lives striving for money."

Streets and shops passed by, slowly or rapidly, depending on the traffic.

"This was such as green and pleasant land once, now look what you have done to it!"

Rachel didn't answer, there was nothing to say. She felt that she was sitting beside an ancient being, somebody much wiser, much more knowledgeable than she was. A creature, she thought again, out of another era, from another different, but bizarrely co-existing, time.

"You mustn't thing too harshly of Gerallt," Morgana said. Rachel hadn't actually though about him at all, she realised. "His brother, Gruffydd was a renegade. He had too much of a fascination, a liking for human things. Mainly your money I should say. He liked to buy things, all this useless stuff you surround yourself with."

Morgana was silent for a while, but then started talking again as they turned onto the motorway.

"His brother was killed; like a moth he flew too close to the flame. And the things that Gerallt did were out of that loyalty he felt to his family. He was wrong, but one can understand the conflict of allegiances."

Just when Rachel though Morgan was being uncharacteristically empathetic, she added:

"Understand, but not forgive."

Rachel saw again the body on the slab. Morgana fell silent and didn't say any more on the subject, but Rachel could join up the dotted lines easily enough. Gwyn and Haf, along with the other fairy women, had spoken of a fairy who had tricked them into coming to London willingly. Perhaps it was this Gruffydd that they had spoken of. It wasn't clear how, or why, he had died. Perhaps he had fallen foul of Andy Francis. And the extent of his brother Gerallt's treachery had yet to be unravelled. But Rachel would happily leave that task to the fairies.

They got to Burnham Beeches early, which Rachel had intended to do, as she wanted to scout the location out, so they had some time to wait. Rachel suggested coffee, but then remembered that Morgana wasn't that fond of the drink. She ended up getting a take-out Americano for herself and a lemonade for Morgana from the cafe. The princess, though was not impressed.

"Everything you humans drink," she said, "tastes unnatural to me."

You're right, Rachel thought to herself, all this stuff is chock full of preservatives and sweeteners, apart from all the refined sugar.

"What will happen to the women that you are taking back?" Rachel asked, as they sat there drinking. "Will they be punished?"

"Why do you care?" Morgana asked. "What are they to you? They're not human!"

What, after all, is human, Rachel asked herself, and what is fairy?

"You said we lived together once. In harmony!"

"Never really harmony, Rachel, just mutual tolerance!"

"Still there must have been some respect then, some mutual sympathy, and that's why I'm asking now. I feel sympathy for those women, human or not!"

"Well, if you are so concerned, I can tell you that the punishment will be minor. They have probably learnt their lesson and will have a cautionary tale to tell."

Rachel didn't push it any further; she wondered, though, what a minor punishment was. Hardly a police caution, she thought, but hopefully 'minor' really meant 'minor' even by human standards.

But then Rachel was distracted, as the Transit van carrying the Inspector, Ceridwen, Rowena and the fairy women was driven into the car park.

"Where are your people?" Rachel asked Morgana and she smiled as she replied:

"All around you!"

They met in the most ludicrous way, on a picnic table, just off to the side of the Common, under the trees near the Visitor's Centre.

"We should sit down," Rachel said. "It will look less suspicious."

Ceridwen and the Inspector sat at one side of the table and Rachel and Morgana on the other. Rachel was tempted to offer them all ice cream, but the two fairy women were looking at each other intensely, if not exactly with outright hostility, and the atmosphere was too serious for such levity.

"Are you well, cousin?" Morgana eventually asked.

"Well enough, cousin," Ceridwen answered. "I hope you are in good health also!"

The exchange – more of a polite convention than a real enquiry - seemed to mark the limit of their conversation and everyone became silent, until eventually the Inspector said:

"Your subjects await, you, Princess! But first we need to talk."

Rachel could see that the Ford Mondeo had just drawn up by the Transit, followed by the rather decrepit mini bus. Both sides stood ready, but no-one would make a move until a signal was given. Morgana was giving the Inspector that enigmatic cat smile, which could mean anything.

"There are things we need to discuss. Firstly, the women. They are returning of their own free will and I hope you will bear in mind that they were tricked by one of their own kind."

That was all the Inspector said about the fairy women; he knew that he shouldn't press that matter further.

"The other matter is that of the Francis gang. We have respected the Treaty and delivered these women up to you, so I'm asking you to respect the Treaty also and leave Andy Francis to us."

Morgana's smile didn't falter.

"I'll bear what you say in mind, Inspector James," she answered.

The dog walkers and day-trippers that were the only other denizens of the car park gave them a few curious looks, but this was England and people generally kept themselves to themselves. Perhaps, Rachel thought, they believed that the van was full of asylum seekers or refugees, but if so, nobody reacted. Perhaps people were more sympathetic than Rachel had previously thought.

The fairy women all went quietly, accepting their fate. After all, there wasn't really anywhere else for them to go. Gwyn and Haf were the last ones out of the Transit. Gwyn had been helping one of the other women – a young frail thing that seemed on the point of fainting – and she looked tired, her face drawn and exhausted.

"I'm sorry, Gwyn," Rachel said, thinking she owed her something, if only words.

"I think it's my fate," Gwyn said, "so there wasn't anything you could have done."

She looked for Haf, found her and took her hand. Rachel noticed that none of Morgana's party had actually talked to the women and hoped that this wasn't an augur of things to come. Rowena and Ceridwen kept at a discreet distance, as there was too much bad blood between them and Morgana's people.

Soon Morgana's band was all in the cars or the minibus, but the princess herself hung back.

"Well, Rachel, I'll say farewell to you now," she said. "I doubt if we'll meet again."

Rachel didn't know what to say; "nice to have met you" didn't seem quite appropriate.

"Have a safe journey, Princess!" She said, instead.

Morgana smiled, as she opened the rear door of the Mondeo, where Elis was waiting for her.

"Are you sure you don't want to come with me?" She asked, not waiting for an answer, smiling again. "You'd have enjoyed serving me!"

Then the car door slammed and the Mondeo pulled out of the space, followed by the mini bus, with the Rover bringing up the rear. Behind a window, Gwyn raised a hand in farewell and Rachel reciprocated. Then the war band of the Cimbriani departed, their mission accomplished, on the way back to their kingdom under the hill.

"Let's hope that's the end of it," Inspector James said. He was beside her and Rowena and Ceridwen were approaching.

"Why wouldn't it be?" Rachel asked.

"Because I was trying to get Morgana to agree to leave the Francis clan to us, but unfortunately she didn't. She was, in fact, very non-committal."

"Fairies can be diplomatic too, as you see," Ceridwen said. "Fairies tend not to lie or break their promises, so they don't give them lightly!"

"Well, we've done all we can," the Inspector said. "And I don't know about anyone else, but I think I need a drink!"

The others started walking towards the Transit, but Rachel spent a few moments looking in the direction of the departing minibus. She could still see Gwyn's face in her mind's eye; a face devoid of hope.

She had one drink and then went back to Ellen. But Ellen wasn't home – Rachel remembered that this was the night she went to the gym after work – so Rachel tidied up and then got dinner together. It was a green salad, a potato salad and a supermarket quiche, but at least she was making an effort. It was all ready when Ellen came in through the door, the wine was open and the table laid.

"What's all this in aid of?" Ellen asked. "Have you got something to tell me? Are you moving out? Getting married again?"

"No," Rachel answered. "It's just that you're always cooking and cleaning up and I'm feeling a bit guilty. And I haven't been around much lately!"

They sat down to eat together – all civilised, Rachel thought, without the TV on – and chatted amiably, but slightly awkwardly.

After they had finished, they sat on the sofa to finish the wine and Ellen suddenly said:

"You know, Rachel, I had the strangest dream last night..."

Chapter 23

Rachel was sitting at her desk, looking at the screen of her P.C. when the desk sergeant rang her to say that she had a visitor. She knew, of course, that it was the Inspector, but, in truth, she had almost forgotten that he was due.

The morning had been spent in the midst of what Andrews called 'firefighting', which in this context meant explaining the inexplicable and covering his and her backs. The worse part of it had been an interview with the Detective Chief Inspector running the Major Incident Team, put in place after the Hav killings. The DCI was one of those women of a certain age who don't so much wear their hearts on their sleeves, but rather their ambitions. And the sleeves are of the well-tailored expensive kinds that go with the well-tailored suit, shoes that cost the equivalent of two months' salary – for Rachel, that is - and impeccably styled hair.

DCI Hughes – "call me Jackie" – was one of those women who were all soft and sensitive and sisterly with you, until they decided to pull rank and jerk you upright like a puppet on a string. It was evident to Rachel that the DCI was on a fishing expedition. She was trying to get Rachel to give her something on her boss, something tangible that could explain the almighty cock-up that had descended on the station.

Because the truth was that there existed a veritable trail of bodies, starting at the Hav, moving onto the canal dock and then ending in Epping Forest. And these were just the human ones. There was also the mysterious "East European" body that had disappeared from the morgue and a similar disappearing body from Epping Forest – Rachel surprised herself with how pleased she was that Morgana had spirited that second body away. The murders themselves would put the Division's crime figures through the roof, which was bad news for everyone. And the fact that there had been armed skirmishes all over the Borough would do nothing for public confidence and the on-going gentrification of the area, which was supposed to be an economic panacea that would solve all the Council's social and economic problems. All in all, it was a 'lose, lose' situation.

DCI Hughes had ushered her into the office that she had purloined – one of the best – for the duration of the enquiry and she had sat Rachel down on one of two easy chairs fronting a coffee table. She took the other.

"I hope that you are feeling okay, Rachel," Call-Me-Jackie said, all care and consolation.

Rachel couldn't at first figure out what she was referring to and then remembered. Of course, it was the shooting at the canal dock.

"You should take some time off and there's usually mandatory counselling in these situations. I hope D.I. Andrews will get you up to speed with all that when he's fully recovered."

Rachel assured her that she was alright and that everything was, and would be, alright; a list of bland, banal reassurances. Then DCI Hughes leant back in her chair and gave Rachel a silent, appraising look. Eventually, she spoke.

"Looking at this case, Rachel, I sometimes get the feeling that I'm trying to put together a jig-saw and though I've got a lot of the pieces, I've never actually seen the picture on the box. Do you understand what I mean?"

Rachel said she did and agreed that the case was puzzling, complex, enigmatic even.

"I don't know if you really do understand me, Rachel. What I mean is that I think someone has seen that picture on the box, that they've actually got the picture, but they are not sharing it."

Rachel didn't answer. There was a file on the table in a manila folder. DCI Hughes spent some time flicking through it.

"You disappeared on assignment for a number of days recently, just in the middle of things." She said, looking up.

"It was just after your team had taken over the case," Rachel nearly added Ma'am, thought of adding Jackie, but instead just tailed off. "I was assigned to aid an Inspector James from a special operations unit based in South Wales."

DCI Hughes nodded and said:

"Nobody's telling me much about that, Rachel. Some sort of internal intelligence work, is all I'm getting. And, by the way, I know that you can't say any more about it yourself."

That was relief, thought Rachel, intelligence work, threat to the realm, was always a get-out-of-gaol-free card. As long as you played it right and didn't end up back in gaol again, pretty damn quickly.

Call-Me-Jackie went back to flicking through the file, but then suddenly looked up at Rachel.

"What's the connection between DI Andrews and Deborah Francis?" She asked.

Rachel knew it was coming. Lull you into a false sense of security, she thought, then hit you with a hard question.

"DI Andrews and I met with Deborah Francis at her home address following a report of a missing person, her husband Tony. Subsequently she informed us that it was a mistake. He wasn't actually missing."

"That's clear, Rachel, from your report, but what I don't understand is why you both went to Mrs. Francis house on spec like that. The husband had only just been reported missing!"

"DI Andrews and I both agreed that if Tony Francis had been abducted, it could have had consequences. We were concerned that it might have led to retaliation and escalation."

"Quite a presumption to make, Rachel. You are sure you both reached that conclusion, it wasn't just Andrews."

Rachel told her that it was a mutual decision, which, she thought, was the truth, or near as damn it. Misleading people, she thought, is always easier, if you tell them half the truth.

DCI Hughes nodded and smiled at Rachel. The smile said: you haven't done anything wrong, you aren't under suspicion. But you might be, it hinted, if you don't co-operate.

"Did DI Andrews meet Mrs. Francis any other times, with you, or without you?"

"With me, no! Without me, I couldn't say!"

"But you met Deb Francis twice, according to your notes, didn't you?"

Rachel swallowed. She was prepared for this line of questioning, but she still disliked dissembling, especially to a senior officer. She'd always been as straight as a die before all this.

"The first time I met her, she contradicted her earlier story and said that her husband had been abducted, by persons unknown. I met her the second time for more information, but I became aware of a potential threat to her safety and my own safety, so I called for back-up."

"And DI Andrews posted a car at your home address for additional protection, didn't he?"

"That was to do with my secondment to the Special Operations Unit, Ma'am," Rachel answered. Let's keep it formal, she thought, no more Call-Me-Jackie.

DCI Hughes sighed and flicked through the folder on the table some more.

"It's all very confusing, Rachel, frustrating even. I suspect that there's much more to all this than you can or want to tell me."

She closed the file and sat back, looking at Rachel, as if expecting her to break the silence.

"You can go, Detective Sergeant!" She said, finally, her voice changed, all sympathy gone, pulling rank.

Rachel stood up and crossed to the door.

"One more thing before you go, DS Stevens!" DCI Hughes said. Rachel turned around and looked at her.

"Be careful that you don't get hung out to dry, Rachel! People will be looking for scapegoats!"

She met the Inspector by the reception desk and, as he stood up from his chair, said to him:

"Shall we take a walk? I think I need to get out of the office for a while!"

It was a sunny, warm day, so they decided to take a turn around the park. The Inspector, despite the heat of the sun, had his standard grey top-coat on, over a suit, and was carrying his walking stick. He just looked like an old man out for a walk; a retired teacher perhaps, quite innocuous really, Rachel thought.

As they walked she told him about the interview with DCI Hughes.

"She's just angry and frustrated, Rachel. You know what our colleagues are like! They hate being kept in the dark about things. And she's got an inkling that you know more than she does. A lowly DS knowing more than a DCI, perish the thought!"

Rachel couldn't help laughing. The Inspector had transcended all this; he obviously didn't care for rank, or convention, perhaps not even the law, or at least the law as it was written.

They found a bench and sat down.

"Ceridwen and Rowena left early in the Transit, but I have some things to do in London, so I'll go back on the train later."

Rachel couldn't help asking what business he had; she was quite intrigued by it.

"I have superiors of a sort, too, Rachel. I have to go down to Whitehall to make a report on this whole incident. There is a file, somewhere, a tome or a book; perhaps they've even digitised it by now. But it's top-secret – on a need-to-know basis – and very people actually need to know.

"Does the Prime Minister know?" Rachel asked. "You know, about the fairies and everything!"

The Inspector shook his head and said:

"Oh no, Rachel, you couldn't tell Prime Ministers this sort of thing, it would scare them too much!"

Rachel laughed again and wondered whether, or not, he was joking. She'd forgotten that the Inspector was such good company; charming and funny, like a fond, old uncle. And not the creepy kind of fond, old uncle, at that.

"I wanted to ask you about Ceridwen," she said, "Morgana called her cousin when they met."

"Well, they are. Cousins, I mean," the Inspector said.

"They know each other!"

"More by repute, really, I suspect. They may have met before, I'm not sure. All those fairy royals are related in some way, however distant. Much like the human European royal families, they are all second cousins once removed and so on."

So Ceridwen was a princess too, Rachel reflected. Though, it should be said, she thought, that Fairy Princesses bore no resemblance to Disney Princesses; they'd gut you as soon as look at you.

"You are, in fact, Rachel, one of the few in the know. About the fairies, I mean! And one of an even lesser number who have actually confronted them in the flesh. That knowledge can be a burden; it can make you see the world differently, make it a more magical place, but also a more frightening realm."

The Inspector looked at his watch and stood up.

"I must get going," he said. "But you know where I am if you need to speak to me or see me. You are one of us now, you know. As I said, one of the few."

He paused, as if thinking, and then added:

"I've got a feeling that we'll be seeing each other again soon!"

They shook hands, a formal goodbye, and then he walked off. She watched him go, a dapper, tidy figure, somehow out of sync with the modern world around him.

Chapter 24

Rachel felt a sense of déjà-vu, as she and Andrews parked just opposite Deb's house. It was just over four weeks before that they'd done exactly the same thing, parked in the same spot on the quiet suburban street, seen the same twitching curtains, a glimpse of neighbours' faces. It was only some fifteen days since that last meeting with the Inspector. So much had happened in those four weeks; her world had been almost turned upside down.

She looked at Andrews besides her. His face still looked bruised and there remained a tracery of cuts on it; it leant him a rakish air. All his injuries had been superficial – the wound on his arm was the worst – and he was supposed to be on sick leave. But Andrews didn't do sick leave. He didn't just work at the job. He was the job; it was his existence.

Rachel's sense of déjà-vu was only increased by the reason they were here. A Francis brother had gone missing again; Andy this time. Her initial reaction - like Andrews' and most the rest of the nick – had been "good riddance", a sense of initial release, then came the surfacing of an underlying anxiety. Because a vacuum at the centre of a criminal enterprise like the Francis Empire always caused chaos and calamity. Deb had called the station that morning and insisted on talking to Andrews. This time Andy had been missing for 48 hours, so it was a legitimate missing person enquiry.

When Deb opened the door, she seemed pleased to see Andrews, but disappointed when she saw that Rachel was with him. Lucky for him, Rachel thought, because Deb looked like she wanted to eat Andrews whole, then and there.

Deb showed them into the sitting room. Rachel noticed she was wearing a little, black dress, accessorised with her standard gold jewelry – too much to be tasteful – and she smelled good and gave off a sun-kissed aura, all tanned smooth skin and sun-bleached hair. It was probably from a bottle or a sun bed, but effective nevertheless.

"Donald, I'm glad you came," she said, when they were sitting down. Deb was in an armchair and Andrews and Rachel were on the sofa. The boss was doing his best to keep his distance, Rachel noticed, trying to foster a professional sense of detachment.

"You'd better tell us what happened, Deb!" Andrews said. Rachel got her note book out.

Andy, apparently, had had to go up to Oxford for the weekend for business of one sort or another. He'd been staying in the Randolph Hotel. He was out of London, so relaxed about his security with only a driver accompanying him. The driver had left him in the bar, talking to a woman.

"Ralph, the driver," Deb said, "told me that Andy had basically sent him away. He was chatting up this woman and Ralph knew where it was leading. But when he knocked on his door in the morning, Andy wasn't there and his bed hadn't been slept in."

"Did he describe the woman?" Rachel asked. Deb looked at her, as if just seeing her for the first time.

"Slim, elegant, foreign-looking," Deb said, a hint of exasperation in her voice.

"Wearing a hat?" Rachel asked.

"What's that got to do with it?" Deb asked in turn, genuinely bemused.

"Nothing," said Rachel. "It doesn't matter."

There wasn't much more that Deb could add.

"You've got my card, Deb," Andrews said, as he stood up to go, "phone me if Ralph remembers anything else or you have more news!"

By the flash of the eyes that Deb shot Andrews, Rachel knew that she'd been on the phone to him by the end of the day, on any pretext.

"How's Tony?" Rachel asked. "How's he doing?"

Deb turned towards her and looked her up and down; she was angry, Rachel could see it.

"He's in a private clinic. The Doctor said he'd needed a calm place to rest and recover. He keeps getting dreams! Flashbacks!"

"Still! At least you got him back," Rachel said.

"Yes! But you never caught them, did you? You let me down, didn't you? I co-operated with you, after all!"

It was Rachel's turn to get annoyed, now.

"Deb, you tried to lure me into a trap! Andy's men would have grabbed me, if I hadn't figured it out!"

Deb looked at her, calculation clear in her eyes, and then she put her hands over her face and started crying. Andrews gave Rachel a withering look and put his arm around Deb's shoulder.

"Come on, Deb. Don't upset yourself!"

Deb looked up at Andrews; Rachel could have sworn she was actually batting her eyelids.

"I'm sorry, Donald. I'm just so overwhelmed by everything!"

As they got back in the car, Andrews looked over at Rachel.

"You were a bit hard on her, weren't you Rachel?" He asked.

"She's a calculating bitch, boss!"

Andrews laughed.

"Yes, that was quite a performance wasn't it? And I don't think she's too upset about Andy."

"No," Rachel said. "I think we know who'll be running the Francis family business from now on!"

"And I think," Andrews said, "We know what happened to Andy!"

"We should get the police in Oxford on it, if they're not already. But he's long gone!"

Rachel knew what they would see on the hotel CCTV, a woman with that innocent, ethereal beauty, which was so attractive to men like Andy. She'd be well-dressed, attentive, would laugh at all his jokes, her voice having a musical quality, like streams flowing, brooks babbling, that drove him wild with passion and desire. And then she would lead him off to his doom.

Chapter 25

This time, the train journey was familiar to Rachel and Abermannan had a more welcoming aspect. It was no longer that god-forsaken place at the end of the line. It was still scruffy with a down-at-heel air of gentility, but it felt familiar. Like a seaside town you had visited on holiday when you were a child and of which you couldn't help but have fond memories, however much it had changed.

And, technically, Rachel thought, she could just about say that she was on holiday. Because she'd done what DCI Hughes had suggested and taken some leave. It had, however, been Andrews who had done most of the persuading, because, as was always the case, she had been reluctant to leave the office.

"You've been through a lot, Rachel," he'd said and she considered, really, that he didn't know the half of it. "You were abducted, for goodness sake, involved in a fire-fight. And you've seen and heard things that you, and most people, aren't supposed to."

Andrews himself had just returned to work. He was on what they called a "phased return", but he seemed be as busy as ever. But when she pointed this out, he would brook no argument.

"You were much more involved in this affair than me, Rachel, and you need to recharge your batteries and try and get the thing in perspective, if that's even possible. There's no counsellor you could go to. No health professional who wouldn't get you sectioned you if you told them what you knew."

In the end, she took his advice. She knew that, in part, he was trying to get rid of her for a spell, while he dealt with the fall-out from what they now euphemistically called "the Havana Nights affair". If Rachel was on sick leave, she couldn't be easily interviewed, and Andrews could do his best to put over his own interpretation of what had happened, without the chance or risk of being contradicted.

It had now been set down in all the reports as a gang war. The trafficking of sex workers was at the heart of it – because, Rachel reiterated, the best lies were always half-truths - but the women had become conveniently vague and Eastern European. Everyone, of course, knew that the Francis clan and their foot soldiers were involved and their opponents were mooted to be a Roma gang. Organised crime from the former Soviet Bloc was still something of an unknown quantity, so an exotic, nomadic criminal organisation, with a taste for using distinct weaponry, such as machetes and hunting crossbows, was a convenient scapegoat, even if it was stretching plausibility to its limits.

Rachel thought that the criminologists and sociologists would have a field day with the case; she envisaged a series of learned articles, in journals that no-one read, analysing this new criminal phenomenon and how it related to the status quo. The tabloid newspapers had, of course, got hold of it and were using it as ammunition in their continuing demonization of immigrants and their monstering of the EU.

"Roma gang fights pitched battle in North London," was one of the less alarmist headlines. Along with the more subtle offerings of "gypsies, tramps and thieves," and "when two tribes go to war", as if someone was plundering a dictionary of song titles.

Rachel had never thought that she'd have willingly co-operated in a cover-up before. She'd always taken a pride in the fact that she was straight and incorruptible, unlike some of the older officers, veterans of the bad old days, whose dubious reputations hung around them like a bad smell. But, for once, she could see that some things had to remain hidden. It was like finding out that the monster under the bed was real; it was better not to tell your kids that, even if you knew it.

Rachel suspected that it was also convenient for Andrews to have Rachel out of commission for a time, because he was still seeing Deb Francis. She had no real proof of this, but there were the phone calls that would interrupt meetings; the way that he would disappear on his own at odd hours and other little tell-tales signs. He was, for instance, taking much more care with the way he dressed and his personal grooming. Rachel, being a veteran of a marriage and an unfaithful husband, knew all these signs. She didn't care that much, but, after all, Deb wasn't just some random bored housewife, she was a spoke in the wheel of a major criminal enterprise, if not its hub, and Andrews was taking some risk in getting involved with her. But that was typical Andrews, Rachel thought, careful and professional at work, but reckless as hell in his personal life.

It hadn't been until she'd got home after her talk with Andrews that she'd realised that he was right; she did need time off. Things had taken a greater toll from her than she'd thought. It was as if that solid ground that she'd always stood on had suddenly tilted and put her off-balance. As if life had suddenly slipped out of the firm grasp with which she had always held it. Inspector James had warned her that encounters with fairies always had consequences, not always direct and immediate, and she wondered if this after-shock was what she was feeling.

She was, though, more worried about Ellen than herself. Ever since Morgana had put the glamour on her, the woman was subject to vivid, colourful dreams, which interrupted her sleep. At first Ellen had described these reveries to her – visions you might call them – of caverns and rivers that ran underground and glittering, crystal caves that resounded with a subtle, haunting music. But, after a while, Ellen would no longer talk to her about these nightly phantasms. Instead, Rachel would come home to find her sitting on the settee staring into space, as if unaware of her surroundings, as if lost in another place. So, Rachel had not just come to Abermannan for herself. She needed to know what to do about Ellen; how to help her.

She took a taxi to the old hospital and avoided the questions of the rather garrulous taxi driver, who tried to find out why she was there. Yes, she was on business. No, she didn't need a hotel or the name of a restaurant. She just needed a ride to her destination. In the end, she told him she was a police officer and that shut him up.

She was almost glad to see to see the glowering receptionist; almost felt a nostalgic twinge at the woman's blank hostility. This was the world – the room, the space – in which she could actually talk about what she had seen, admit it, and deal with it in some way. It felt strangely liberating, like, she imagined, an alcoholic's first A.A. meeting.

"I'm very pleased to see you, D.S. Stevens," Inspector James said as he greeted her formally, with a handshake.

He hadn't kept her waiting for long; it was as if he had been expecting her. He made them coffee – real coffee, in a press – and put out a plate of biscuits, which neither of them touched.

His office, Rachel saw, was on the top floor of the building – up in the eaves – and had a view of the bay beyond, through a rather magnificent circular window. The walls were lined with wooden shelves holding books and files and the Inspector's desk – a massive, oaken object – looked like it had been in situ since the building opened its doors as a hospital in the 1900s.

"I hear you took some leave," he said, when they were sitting either side of his desk. "I also hear that Andy Francis has gone missing."

"I think we both know what happened to him," Rachel said.

They drank the coffee and then the Inspector suggested some lunch. They left his office and crossed the road to a cafe, an amazingly old-fashioned place, where everything seemed to come with chips, even the salad. They had fish with their chips – it was fresh and locally landed, the Inspector told her – and then took a turn around a small park that looked towards the coast, divided from the sands by the main road and a promenade. She could feel the breeze off the sea, almost taste the salt in the air. Overhead, gulls rode on the wind, as she told the Inspector about Ellen and her dreams.

"Fairies have a strange psychological effect on the people they come into contact with – especially those they put under a glamour – and, as you would no doubt suspect, it's not an area into which much research has been done."

The sun was pleasantly warm, so they sat for a time of a park bench, watching mothers pushing prams, a few old people out for a stroll and office workers escaping the daily grind to eat their lunch in the open air.

"Is there anything I can do?" Rachel asked. She felt that she had got Ellen into this. It was all her fault after all.

"You can wait!" The Inspector said. "That may work. The memories – disturbances, or dreams, whatever you call them – may recede. Or you can tell her!"

"Wouldn't that make it worse?" Rachel asked.

"Not necessarily!" The Inspector replied. "Sometimes the truth can come as a relief, however bizarre it might be."

They walked back to the Inspector's office. Rachel realised they hadn't really talked about the subject she had actually come to discuss; what to do about Andy Francis?

"Do you think he is still alive?" Rachel asked.

"Oh, undoubtedly, I would say," the Inspector answered, not having to ask who she meant. "Morgana will keep him alive in a dungeon somewhere. If he doesn't actually go insane, he will eventually lose any sense of who he is. His former life will seem unreal, like a dream."

There was a strange tone in the Inspector's voice as he said this, wistful or sad, but also strangely personal. As if he had experienced that which he spoke of.

"You remember that I did warn him about it and he scoffed at the warning. I told him that he didn't know what he was dealing with or the potential dangers."

Rachel well remembered what the Inspector had said to Andy Francis in the interview room, when his lawyer had been lured away, but at the time, when Andy had virtually laughed in the old man's face, even Rachel hadn't totally believed him.

"Can't we do anything?" She asked.

"Well, not unless we want a full-scale war with Faerie. And I shudder to think what that would involve or where it would end."

"But isn't it covered by the Treaty you are always quoting?"

The Inspector stopped and smiled at her when she said this.

"Yes, I do tend to bang on about it, don't I?"

They walked on.

"The thing is, Rachel, if we wanted to invoke the Treaty, we would have to prosecute Andy Francis and anyone else involved in the trafficking of the women and the deaths of Morgana's people. Frankly, I can't see that happening, can you?"

Rachel considered what the Inspector had said. She knew he was right. It was better to give up on Andy Francis, leave him to Morgana's form of justice. This was out of the parameters of human law, a good way out.

They were back at the office now. The Inspector ushered her past the receptionist who, as usual, frowned at her.

"I must apologise, Rachel, but I have a meeting in ten minutes, so I'll have to leave you, but Rajma is here and wants to see you."

"I won't take up any more of your time, Inspector," Rachel said, "but I was just wondering if there was anything we could do for those two fairy women, Gwyn and Haf."

"What do you suggest, Rachel? Even if we could persuade Morgana to release them, where do they think they could go?"

"What about here?" Rachel asked.

"Do you think we could take in every fairy exile or dissident? Every one of them who tires of the strictures of that life for some reason?"

Rachel didn't answer. She knew that it was a nearly insurmountable problem. She stood up to go, but the Inspector stopped her, saying:

"We've got five minutes, Rachel. I think there might just be a way around this, so let me tell you what I think we can do."

Rajma was in her office, which wasn't as impressive as the Inspector's, having one narrow window, which looked over an overgrown, enclosed courtyard. It did however, have a PC and a modern-looking phone, not like the antique on the Inspector's table, which looked as if it had been hand-crafted by Alexander Graham Bell.

"I knew we'd see you soon," Rajma said when she saw her. "Once you've stumbled into this world, it's hard to stay away."

"I'm on leave, actually," Rachel answered, a little piqued, "so it's not really official business."

"Well, you wouldn't exactly call any of our business official!" Rajma replied and Rachel had to laugh.

"Have you had lunch?" Rajma asked.

"Fish and chips," Rachel answered, adding: "Very nice too!" Just in case the café was the unit's regular lunchtime venue.

"Don't tell me! The full Windsor Caff workout! I was going to suggest an ice cream down at the pier, but not if you're stuffed."

"I think I have got room for an ice cream," Rachel said. "I am sort-of on holiday!"

The drive was familiar; they were heading for the village at the end of the bay where the Inspector lived. Rajma found a parking spot down by the sea-front and they strolled along the promenade, getting ice-cream at a kiosk and enjoying the afternoon sun.

"How are the all the troops?" Rachel asked and it took a moment for Rajma to fathom what she meant.

"Oh, they're fine. Rowena and Ceridwen have just come back from a job in Cornwall, so they're taking a couple of days off."

"Trouble with the Pixies?" Rachel asked.

"They're a troublesome lot!" Rajma answered.

"No, seriously?" Rachel asked. "I was joking!"

"So was I," Rajma said. But Rachel wasn't totally sure.

"Carreg isn't the sort of person who can happily inhabit an office," Rajma went on. "He keeps to his little cottage in the country and the Inspector calls him in when he is needed. He can't go back to his people, but we keep him busy enough."

Rachel didn't ask who Carreg's people were. She had enough to deal with already – fairies were sufficiently time consuming - without delving into any other supernatural races.

"How did you get into this... this line of work?" Rachel asked Rajma as they walked back to the car.

"I saw a Djinn when I was a teenager. The creature appeared to me and tried to lure me away from my family. I ended up being referred to a psychiatrist and hospitalised. On medication. But my Imam contacted the Inspector and he knew what to do."

They were in the car now, but Rajma didn't make a move to start it.

"The Inspector knew an old man who was an Islamic scholar, an expert in the field. They confronted the Djinn, which everyone else said was a figment of my imagination, and broke his hold over me. Which is why I'm here today. And I don't only mean working for the unit! That's why I'm alive and sane!"

They were silent for a few moments, as Rachel let Rajma's words sink in. She almost felt that she had intruded, asked one question too far. But after a short time, Rajma smiled at her and then reached out and squeezed her hand.

"I don't mind you asking, Rachel, really! It's good that you know."

"There's one other thing that's been intriguing me," Rachel said. "Morgana's second-in-command said that the Inspector was married to one of the Fair Folk."

"Yes, Rachel, he is!" Rajma said. "And I think you saw her!"

"She was in the house all the time that I was there!"

"Yes..." Rajma replied. "And no!"

Rachel looked puzzled.

"I'm not being obtuse, Rachel. I think you already know that fairies can and do occupy time and space in a different way to us. So, the Inspector's wife is there sometimes and is not there at other times. He doesn't even know himself when she decides to visit!"

"But it wasn't like that with Morgana!"

"You're right, Rachel, but fairies – some of them, at least - can effectively choose how they move through space and time. It accounts, really for their longevity."

"It makes for a difficult marriage, doesn't it?"

"More complicated than you know!"

Rajma turned the key in the ignition.

"Let's get you back to the station," she said. "Otherwise you'll miss your train."

Rajma took her to the train and saw her off on the platform. Just as Rachel stepped up into the carriage, she put an envelope into her hand.

"Open this on the train, Rachel!" She said. Then they hugged briefly, the guard started closing the doors and soon the train pulled out of the station gathering speed. Rachel sat down in her seat, putting the envelope on the table in front of her. She opened it and saw that there was a Post-It attached to a more formal document.

"Dear Rachel," the Post-It read. "Do you want to come and work with us?" It was signed by Inspector James Ellis James.

Who'd have thought it, Rachel mused, what unimaginative parents?

The Post-It was attached to a letter, which was basically a request for Andrews to second her to the Inspector's unit for an unspecified period. Written on the Post-It there was a P.S. under the Inspector's name. "You decide! If you want to take up the offer, just give the letter to DI Andrews."

Chapter 26

It was a long drive to Keswick - exhausting actually, there was so much motorway - and by the time she came to the Lake District she was too jaded to appreciate the scenery. She'd booked into a small hotel. She didn't bother to eat dinner, but got fish and chips from a takeaway and a bottle of wine from a local corner shop.

Contacting Morgana hadn't been straightforward – fairies didn't have postal addresses, after all, or email – but there were channels, of course, which the Inspector was well-versed in using. There were go-betweens, it turned out, messengers; shadowy figures who moved between the two worlds. Rachel never knew the details of the transaction, but a message was sent and eventually a date, time and location came back.

Rachel spent the morning walking around Keswick, feeling like a fish out of water in her city coat and city shoes. She really felt she should buy a waterproof and a pair of walking boots and cap it all off with a sensible, but slightly garish, hat of some sort. In truth the town seemed full of people in walking gear – most of it suspiciously pristine and clean, as if the wearers had more money than any actual inclination to ramble.

She found the coffee shop easily enough. Sitting there with an Americano at 11am, she thought how pleasant it was to find a good, independent coffee place somewhere like this, instead of the ubiquitous coffee chains that were everywhere. As she sat there in the window, a figure stared in at her. It was hard to think that it was actually Morgana. It looked instead like a slim, young girl, in the standard street uniform of jeans, sweater and jacket. You could really carry off tight jeans if you had that slender, fairy figure, Rachel thought. The only slightly unfashionable detail was the woolly hat pulled down over the ears; the giveaway fairy disguise. Rachel looked around for bodyguards; any suspicious looking figures hanging around shop-fronts or in the mouths of alleyways, but it seemed that Morgana had come alone.

She must trust me, Rachel thought, slightly flattered.

"I thought you didn't like coffee, Princess," Rachel said as Morgana walked in.

"Drop the title, Rachel," Morgana answered, "and I'm having a milk-shake. A chocolate one!"

Rachel ordered the drink, as she knew that princesses were used to giving commands and getting their way.

"What is this about, Rachel? You know I wouldn't have ordinarily met you - no offense - but you used diplomatic channels and I couldn't refuse."

Rachel thought that diplomatic channels sounded a grand way of putting it, but it was true, she knew, that those covert channels of communication between human and fairy depended on mutual respect and response.

"I think you know, Morgana. It's no coincidence that Andy Francis went missing, just after you left London."

Morgana's face took on a set expression.

"Say that I had this person you are talking about. Say that he had been sentenced by me, to be my prisoner for an eternity, to think on what he had done and to act as a warning to others. Say all this was true, then I would not return him and you would not get him back. Even if you came here with an army, I would fight you!"

She relented somewhat and her face softened.

"This is not about the Treaty, Rachel, this is about revenge! Some things have to be paid for!"

The milkshake came, so they fell silent, and then Morgana took a number of long, interminable sips at it.

"That's one human thing I have a taste for," she said. "Chocolate!"

She eyed Rachel again, weighing her up. Rachel cleared her throat and started speaking.

"I was talking with the Inspector about this very matter! And though the Treaty seems very clear on this point – he's read it after all, though I haven't – that human justice is for humans and fairy justice for fairies, there is one exception."

Morgana looked intrigued now.

"What do you mean?" She asked.

"Hostages!" Rachel said.

"Hostages! There hasn't been the need for hostages for hundreds of years. That only happened in the early years of the treaty!"

"I know," Rachel agreed. "The Inspector said as much. But the provision is there."

Morgana was interested, Rachel could see, but a little confused as well.

"If we treat your guest as a hostage under the Treaty, there's no obligation for you to return him or for us to get him back."

"So, what do you want in return, Rachel?" Morgana asked.

"Well, we need a hostage. Or hostages. Willing ones of course!"

"And you obviously had someone in mind!" Morgana said. She was quick on the uptake, Rachel thought.

"There are two women, Haf and Gwyn I think they are called, but I'm not sure of their full names."

"As it happens, I know them well. They have been brought to my attention a number of times!" Morgana had reverted to her usual regal tones.

That sounds ominous, Rachel thought.

"But why should I agree to this? I already have the human. Why should I give up any of my servants, because you ask?"

Morgana was angry now, Rachel could see. She didn't respond well to threats or demands, it was obvious.

"I'm just making a suggestion, Morgana. But isn't that part of being a princess, someone with power, making gracious gestures?"

For a moment Morgana looked as if she would dearly like to strangle Rachel with those slim, fair hands of hers, but then, suddenly, she laughed.

"Oh, you do amuse me, Rachel! I really do think you should come and live me, to liven up the place now and then!"

It sounded more a threat than an invitation and, for a moment, Rachel wondered whether she had made a mistake. Up here, this close to the kingdom of the Cimbriani, she was hopelessly exposed and virtually powerless. She could hardly go the Cumbrian Police and say she was being chased by fairies, after all! But though Rachel felt frisson of fear at the threat of being abducted by Morgana again, there was a part of her that was intrigued by the prospect. What would it be like to look on the halls of those fairy palaces, under the hill, and what would she give to see them? She shook the thought from her head, not willing to entertain it.

Morgana was silent, sipping the milkshake and looking gravely at Rachel through those rather beautiful, green eyes of hers. Eventually, she stopped, wiped her mouth with the back of her hand – not princess behaviour, Rachel thought – and said:

"They were pretty useless anyway, those two – whatever they names are, Gwyn and Haf – even before they ran away to London. And they are no better now. You can have them, my gift to you! On the morrow!"

Rachel was tempted to enlighten Morgana about the immorality of owing other beings, but she kept silent, thinking she had only just got away with it.

Morgana stood up.

"Well, fair Rachel. A kiss goodbye!"

Morgana leaned towards her and though Rachel was loath to let the fairy touch her – she didn't want to be glamoured again – the fairy's lips as they brushed both her cheeks were as light as a butterfly wings.

"The kiss of peace, Rachel, and fare you well until we meet again!"

Then Morgana was gone as quickly as she had come.

Rachel realised, as she walked through the streets of Keswick, that they had actually made no firm arrangement. She wondered how she could have been so stupid; surely, they should have arranged a time and a venue. But the next morning, when she went down to pay her bill at the hotel reception, the young woman told her that she had visitors and there were Haf and Gwyn sitting there in the lounge, both with small bundles of clothes and possessions, looking frightened and disconcerted. Until, that is, they saw Rachel.

Rachel hurried them out, quietening their greeting and protestations of thanks.

"Let's go before Morgana changes her mind!" Rachel said.

"But where are we going?" Gwyn asked, but she didn't really look that concerned about the destination; rather she was smiling, her face lit up like the morning sun.

"Next stop, Abermannan!" Rachel said. "You are going to love it!"

Printed in Great Britain
by Amazon